THE SAUNDERS SOUND-OFF

WHERE ARE THEY NOW?

Saunders University Keeps Track of Its Notable Alumni

David Westport

Our star player had big dreams of playing for his home team, the Boston Red Sox. Now he's a small-business owner and happily married father of two. Too bad he never went pro—he could have been a legend! Bet he wonders what could have been....

Sandra Taylor Westport

The girl who captured the jock's heart had big dreams of winning a Pulitzer Prize one day. Her writing was everything to her, but now her kids— and the family business—have taken over. Maybe one day she'll get to pick up where she left off, and find the story of a lifetime!

Tune in next month, graduates, when *The Saunders Sound-Off* brings you up to date on more of your old friends!

Dear Reader,

It's hot and sunny in my neck of the woods—in other words, perfect beach reading weather! And we at Silhouette Special Edition are thrilled to start off your month with the long-awaited new book in *New York Times* bestselling author Debbie Macomber's Navy series, *Navy Husband.* It features a single widowed mother; her naval-phobic sister, assigned to care for her niece while her sister is in the service; and a handsome lieutenant commander who won't take no for an answer! In this case, I definitely think you'll find this book worth the wait....

Next, we begin our new inline series, MOST LIKELY TO..., the story of a college reunion and the about-to-be-revealed secret that is going to change everyone's lives. In *The Homecoming Hero Returns* by Joan Elliott Pickart, a young man once poised for athletic stardom who chose marriage and fatherhood instead finds himself face-to-face with the road not taken. In Stella Bagwell's next book in her MEN OF THE WEST series, *Redwing's Lady,* a Native American deputy sheriff and a single mother learn they have more in common than they thought. *The Father Factor* by Lilian Darcy tells the story of the reunion between a hotshot big-city corporate lawyer who's about to discover the truth about his father—and a woman with a secret of her own. If you've ever bought a lottery ticket, wondering, if just once, it could be possible...be sure to grab *Ticket to Love* by Jen Safrey, in which a pizza waitress from Long Island is sure that if *she* isn't the lucky winner, it must be the handsome stranger in town. Last, new-to-Silhouette author Jessica Bird begins THE MOOREHOUSE LEGACY, a miniseries based on three siblings who own an upstate New York inn, with *Beauty and the Black Sheep.* In it, responsible sister Frankie Moorehouse wonders if just this once she could think of herself first as soon as she lays eyes on her temporary new chef.

So keep reading! And think of us as the dog days of August begin to set in....

Toodles,

Gail Chasan
Senior Editor

Please address questions and book requests to:
Silhouette Reader Service
U.S.: 3010 Walden Ave., P.O. Box 1325, Buffalo, NY 14269
Canadian: P.O. Box 609, Fort Erie, Ont. L2A 5X3

THE HOMECOMING HERO RETURNS

JOAN ELLIOTT PICKART

Silhouette®

SPECIAL EDITION®

Published by Silhouette Books

America's Publisher of Contemporary Romance

For our editor, Susan Litman,
who survived this challenging project
in spite of us.
Thank you.

Special thanks and acknowledgment are given
to Joan Elliott Pickart for her contribution to
the MOST LIKELY TO... series.

 SILHOUETTE BOOKS

ISBN 0-373-24694-3

THE HOMECOMING HERO RETURNS

Books by Joan Elliott Pickart

Silhouette Special Edition

*Friends, Lovers...and
  Babies! #1011
*The Father of Her Child #1025
†Texas Dawn #1100
†Texas Baby #1141
Wife Most Wanted #1160
The Rancher and the Amnesiac Bride #1204
ΔThe Irresistible Mr. Sinclair #1256
ΔThe Most Eligible M.D. #1262
Man...Mercenary...Monarch #1303
*To a MacAllister Born #1329
*Her Little Secret #1377
Single with Twins #1405
◊The Royal MacAllister #1477
◊Tall, Dark and Irresistible #1507
◊The Marrying MacAllister #1579
◊Accidental Family #1616
The Homecoming Hero Returns #1694

*The Baby Bet
†Family Men
ΔThe Bachelor Bet
◊The Baby Bet: MacAllister's Gifts

Silhouette Desire

*Angels and Elves #961
Apache Dream Bride #999
†Texas Moon #1051
†Texas Glory #1088
Just My Joe #1202
ΔTaming Tall, Dark Brandon #1223
*Baby: MacAllister-Made #1326
*Plain Jane MacAllister #1462

Silhouette Books

*His Secret Son
◊Party of Three
◊Crowned Hearts
  "A Wish and a Prince"

Previously published under the pseudonym Robin Elliott

Silhouette Special Edition

Rancher's Heaven #909
Mother at Heart #968

Silhouette Intimate Moments

Gauntlet Run #206

Silhouette Desire

Call It Love #213
To Have It All #237
Picture of Love #261
Pennies in the Fountain #275
Dawn's Gift #303
Brooke's Chance #323
Betting Man #344
Silver Sands #362
Lost and Found #384
Out of the Cold #440
Sophie's Attic #725
Not Just Another Perfect Wife #818
Haven's Call #859

JOAN ELLIOTT PICKART

is the author of over eighty-five novels. When she isn't
writing, Joan enjoys reading, gardening and attending
craft shows on the town square with her young daughter,
Autumn. Joan has three all-grown-up daughters and three
fantastic grandchildren. Joan and Autumn live in a charming small town in the high pine country of Arizona.

Dear David,

You are the coolest guy in school and the <u>best</u> boyfriend a girl could ask for! This has been the <u>best</u> year—especially the homecoming weekend. You played better than ever, and I just <u>know</u> you'll be playing for the Red Sox someday—and I'll be the reporter covering the games!☺ I'll never forget our <u>private</u> celebration after the festivities, either. I'm so glad I didn't have to share you with your adoring fans all night.

I love you, baby, and can't wait to see you on the field again next year!

XOXOXOX

Sandra

Chapter One

Sandra Westport slid her hands into puffy mitts, then removed a tray of golden brown cupcakes from the oven. After setting the tray on a wire cooling rack on the counter, she slid another batch into the oven and removed the mitts. Settling onto a chair at the table, she continued the interrupted task of spreading frosting on several dozen of the treats.

She blew a puff of air upward, trying and failing to move the annoying curl of hair that had flopped onto her moist forehead. After swirling the chocolate frosting into place she set the cupcake to the side and picked up another, just as her husband entered the kitchen.

"Oh-h-h, I'm a dying man," David Westport gasped. "You could fry an egg on those sidewalks out there."

He bent over, placed his hands on his knees and took several deep breaths before straightening again.

"Come here, lovely wife," he said, flinging out his arms, "and give me a big hug."

Sandra laughed. "Not on your life, buster. You are a soggy, sweaty, icky mess. Take a shower and I may reconsider your request. Anyone who goes running in Boston in July is cuckoo, sir. I think the humidity is as high as the temperature and it's only a little after 8:00 a.m. Grim, very grim."

David chuckled and crossed the kitchen to retrieve a bottle of water from the refrigerator, which he chugalugged. He came back to stand next to the table.

"The sanity of a woman who bakes in this weather might be in question, too, madam," he said, reaching for a cupcake.

"Hey, don't touch those," Sandra said. "They're for the bake sale at church tomorrow. Don't even ask where my brain was when I volunteered to do this. There should be a rule that only people who have air-conditioning in their houses should be expected to turn on the oven to donate to these projects."

She sighed and stared into space for a moment. "Air-conditioning. I hear that it's a marvelous invention."

"I heard that rumor, too," David said, snagging a

cupcake and removing the paper cup. "One of these days, my sweet. In the meantime, could you quit bringing it up? I'm tired of hearing about it." He ate the cupcake in two bites. "There. I have performed a public service by taste-testing the goodies, and I must say, that was a superb little cake, Shirley Temple."

Sandra pointed the frosting-covered knife at him.

"Don't start with the Shirley Temple thing, David Westport. You know my hair goes nuts in humidity like this. Maybe I'll get a buzz cut like Michael. I swear, David, our son is never going to forgive me for the fact that he inherited my naturally curly blond hair and Molly got your thick, straight black hair. He'll probably do one of those deals where the kid divorces the parent."

"Speaking of the Westport twins," David said, "I assume they're still sleeping?"

"Yep. It's one of the perks of being ten. You don't get roped into making a zillion cupcakes on a hot and humid day." Sandra paused. "I wasn't nagging about air-conditioning, David."

The timer went off on the stove and Sandra hurried to remove the tray from the oven. She turned the dial to Off, switched the cooled cupcakes with the hot ones and brought the tray to the table.

"Almost done," she said, sinking back onto her chair. "I've lost count here, but there should be enough for the sale and to still have some for us."

"I should hope so," David said, reaching for another one.

"Go away," Sandra said, flicking the knife so a blob of frosting landed on the back of David's hand. "Do the world a favor and take a shower, sweaty man."

"Okay," David said, then proceeded to lick the frosting from his hand.

"Gross," Sandra said, laughing.

"Nothing like a little salty sweat mixed in with chocolate frosting," David said, wrinkling his nose. "Yuck. I'm hittin' the suds."

Sandra shifted in her chair to watch her husband stride from the room.

Good grief, she thought, he was still so gorgeous. They'd been married nearly eleven years and he could still make her heart go pitter-patter. David was tall, dark and handsome, with the added bonus of incredible green eyes. He didn't weigh a pound more than when they'd met in college, kept himself fit and trim. He was just so beautifully proportioned with broad shoulders, narrow waist, muscular legs and…

A coil of heat tightened low in Sandra's body and she spun back around in her chair.

"It's hot enough in here," she said to a cupcake, "without thinking about… Sandra, shut-up."

She continued to frost the cupcakes by rote as her mind wandered.

Every year they went through the same silly ritual, she thought. She'd make wistful comments about having air-conditioning in the house, and David would declare that one of these days, oh, yes, one of these days, they would have the coveted cooling. And both of them knew it would never happen. There just wasn't enough money for a luxury like installing air-conditioning, then paying the bills that running it created. Nope. Not in this lifetime.

Oh, sure, they had AC at the ever-famous Westport's Emporium because it made good business sense. Customers stayed longer and put more groceries and sundry other items into their carts because they were comfortable, in no rush to go back outside into the heat.

"Done," Sandra said, setting the last cupcake on the table.

She got to her feet and went to the small pantry beyond the kitchen to retrieve the plastic carriers she'd use to transport the desserts to the church the next day. As she began to pack the treats, she frowned.

Why had she just wasted mental energy thinking about the air-conditioning they didn't have, would never have? she wondered. She was an intelligent woman, for heaven's sake, a part-time journalistic reporter extraordinaire for the ten-page weekly neighborhood newspaper, the *North End News*. And, yes, sir, by golly, she was hot on the trail of a scoop. After tomorrow she'd turn in an award-winning story on the bake sale that had been held at St. Luke's Episcopal Church after the eleven-o'clock service on Sunday.

"You're losing it, Sandra," she said, snapping the cover onto the first carrier. "You fried your brain when you turned on the oven to bake these messy things."

As she continued her task she inwardly sighed.

Such big dreams she'd had a zillion years ago, she mused. She'd travel the world as a famous journalist with editors clamoring for first chance to publish her genius-level words that flowed effortlessly from her fingertips. Yeah, right.

Sandra swiped her finger around the inside edge of the frosting bowl, then licked the gooey chocolate absently as she stared into space.

Dreams, she thought. She'd long ago tucked hers away and concentrated on her family, her beautiful children, the husband she loved every bit as when they were first married, if not more. She didn't resent for one second that she'd had to forget her career dreams.

But David?

David's potential for success hadn't been a dream, it was a given way back when. He had everything it took to be a professional baseball player and it was simply a matter of graduating from Saunders University where they both went and waiting to see which major league team would draft him. He could have had it all…fame, fortune and a house with air-conditioning.

He'd been close, so very close, to having his dreams come true…but then…she'd gotten pregnant. She had just turned nineteen, was so young and terrified, and she could still remember so clearly weeping buckets while David held her in his arms.

He'd been wonderful, Sandra remembered, as she began to clean up after her baking spree. He'd told her in a voice ringing with conviction that everything would be fine. They'd be married immediately and love and cherish their baby when it was born.

She'd quit college, went to work as a waitress and David found a part-time job pumping gas to help pay the rent on the shabby little apartment they'd found. But everything had *not* been fine. David couldn't keep up the grueling schedule and flunked out of Saunders before he could graduate.

His dreams for being a pro baseball player were buried beneath diapers and bottles and bibs. For *two* babies. Twins. Their beautiful and wondrous Michael and Molly.

And to this day, Sandra thought, as she wiped off the table, she still believed—*knew*—that David resented what had happened, was not truly happy, and definitely did not love her anymore, hadn't loved her for a very long time.

Oh, he put on a smiling facade, was a devoted father, worked hard at the store, gave the impression that he was a man who was contented with his life.

But she couldn't remember, no matter how hard she tried, the last time that David had told her that he loved her.

When would it happen? Sandra wondered, blinking away unwanted tears. When would he have had enough of this charade and leave her? Did he consider ten-years-plus a long enough punishment for a foolish mistake? Oh, dear heaven, what could she do to make him love her again? What, what, what? She loved David so much, couldn't bear the thought of losing him, but she didn't know how to stop it from happening.

"Hi, Mom. I smell cake or cookies or something."

"Oh," Sandra said, grateful to be pulled from her depressing thoughts. "Good morning, Molly mine. I made cupcakes for the bake sale at church tomorrow, but there's some left over for us. You have to have breakfast before you can have one, though."

"Bummer," Molly said, sliding onto a chair at the table. The enormous T-shirt she was wearing as pajamas slid off one shoulder. "I hate breakfast. It's boring."

"How sad," Sandra said, smiling. "Do you think that shirt of your father's is big enough for you?"

"It's cool," Molly said, glancing down at the faded lettering that said Saunders University. "Dad was going to use it to dry the car after he washed it, but I talked him into letting me have it. My friend Becky sleeps in a T-shirt of her dad's that says Harvard, but he never even went there. That's bogus. At least Dad went to Saunders."

But didn't graduate, Sandra thought, inwardly sighing.

"Yep, he did attend Saunders," she said brightly. "So did I for about two seconds. Okay, breakfast. Cereal? Pancakes? Eggs? Your wish is my command. Ah, here's your lazy brother. I can get this cooking number over with in one swoop and exit stage left from this hot kitchen."

"The whole house is hot," Michael said, flopping onto a chair across from Molly. "That shirt you're wearing is so lame, Molly."

"It is not," she said, none too quietly. "You'd have grabbed it in a second if I hadn't seen it first, Michael Westport, and you know it."

"Whoa," Sandra said. "Let's postpone the wars until after you've had some food. What will it be, my sweets?"

"Pancakes," David said, striding into the room, his hair still wet from his shower. "I'm going to make my specialty of blueberry pancakes."

Sandra laughed. "Without the blueberries because we don't have any. I'm going to the grocery store later and will get some. Are there any at the emporium?"

"Nope, they were sold out, but no problem," David said, rubbing his hands together. "I'll make up for the lack of blueberries by making my famous animal-shaped pancakes."

"Cool," Michael said. "I want one huge dinosaur."

"Yuck," Molly said. "I want a lot of nice little butterflies."

"And you, madam?" David said to Sandra.

"Well, let's see," she said, tapping one fingertip on her chin. "A teddy bear, please, sir."

"Got it. Okay, M and M, go get dressed, make your beds and by the time you get back we'll be ready to roll here."

The twins dashed from the room.

"They're so cute," Sandra said. "Ten is a wacky age, isn't it? You've been making animal pancakes since you would put them on their high chair trays and they still think it's super. One minute they try to act so grown up and the next second they're just our babies again."

David started pulling what he needed from the cupboards.

"Yeah," he said, "but they'll be up and grown, then out the door and gone before we know it. I hate the thought of that, I really do, but you can't stop the clock from ticking. When it's time for them to go, they'll go."

A chill swept through Sandra as she stared at David's broad back.

Was that his decision? she thought frantically. Had he made up his mind to grit his teeth and hang in here until the twins left home because he loved them so much? But then it would be time for him to go, too? Dear God, was she destined to lose her whole family at once?

"You know," she said, her voice not quite steady, "I think I'll pass on the pancake, David. I licked the frosting bowl and I really don't want sweet syrup at this point."

"Whatever," David said, beginning to stir the batter in the bowl. "The kids and I will eat your share."

"I'm sure you will. I'm going to go gather the wash."

Sandra hurried from the kitchen. David frowned as he watched her go, then flicked on the radio on the counter and began to sing along off-key to a country and western tune about having friends in low places.

The Westport home was an apartment on the fourth floor of an old brick building. It had the exact same floor plan as every other apartment on their street and several adjacent ones. The eating area was in the kitchen, the door opened directly into a common hallway with no extra frills like a foyer or entryway. The three bedrooms were small, the living room fairly good-sized. There was a laundry room in the basement of the building.

David and Sandra had borrowed the money for the

down payment on the apartment from Sandra's parents when David dropped out of Saunders and had long since paid back the loan. David had gone to work at a nearby grocery store while Sandra continued to wait tables until her doctor told her she had to quit the job and get off her feet if she hoped to carry the twins to term.

When the owner of the grocery store decided to retire three years later he offered David the opportunity to buy the place with reasonable monthly payments. Westport's Emporium had been born and flourished under David's management. He added a great many Italian delicacies as the majority of the citizens residing in the North End of Boston were Italians.

David also broadened the range of what was available to his customers, such as greeting cards, inexpensive gifts for that last minute invitation, supplies needed for barbecuing outside on the fire escape, which was a favorite summer activity in the neighborhood, and other items that a person often needed but didn't want to drive to the larger markets to buy.

The store was doing well, but had reached its financial potential, while the cost of raising two children continued to rise as the twins became active in sports and seemed to outgrow their clothes overnight.

Sandra's part-time job at the newspaper helped the budget some but there never seemed to be money for any extras. Plus, the recent news that both kids were going to need braces on their teeth had caused more than one tossing and turning night for their parents.

As Sandra gathered the wash from the hampers in each bedroom she found herself once again dwelling on the money dilemma. David was still adamant about her not working full-time, wanted her home when the children returned from school each day. Michael and Molly were not going to be latch-key kids no matter how tight the budget became, and she agreed totally with David on the subject.

One possibility David had suggested in the wee hours of a night was to purchase the empty storefront next to the emporium, punch through the wall and expand.

Back in the kitchen, Sandra sorted the wash into piles on the floor, then reloaded the basket.

If they got a loan to purchase the empty building, she thought, they would be so deeply in debt, providing, of course, they could even qualify for the loan in the first place. She'd had a glimmer of hope when David had suggested the idea as it didn't make sense that he would be thinking of expanding the store if he was planning to leave her because he just didn't love her anymore.

But then this morning he'd made that reference to how quickly the twins would be up and gone and she couldn't erase from her mind the image of David following them right out the door when they left.

Oh, David, she thought, wrapping her hands around her elbows. They had been so happy once, so in love, seeing nothing but sunshine and blue skies in each new day. They'd adored their newborn babies, shared the chores connected with twins and ate endless macaroni and cheese dinners while taking turns making up delectable meals they would pretend to be eating.

But at some point—oh, when had it begun?—a distance grew between them. David's focused more and more on the children and the store, hardly seeming to have time for her at all.

It was too many years of just scraping by, she was convinced. Too many. David knew what he could have had as a professional ball player and resented the shattering of his dreams. If he ever forgot what his potential had been, his father was right there ready to remind him, having never forgiven his son for not achieving the goals set for him by the senior Mr. Westport.

"Hanging out with dirty laundry?" David said, poking his head through the doorway.

"What?" Sandra said, as she came back to the moment. "David, when are we going to discuss further the possibility of expanding the store?"

"I'm mulling it over," he said, "and I also want to meet with the accountant and get his opinion."

What about *her* opinion? Sandra thought. David

had never really asked her how she felt about it, had just said it was an idea that had popped into his head and might, or might not, be the answer they were looking for.

"Oh." Sandra nodded. "Well, I thought you and I could sit down and make a list. You know, pro and con. Brainstorm the whole thing...together."

"Yeah, maybe. Listen, I'm taking the kids over to the city pool. Too bad you don't like to swim because it's at least a way to cool off for a while in this weather. Catch you later."

"Bye."

Sandra picked up the laundry basket and only then noted absently that David had cleaned up after the pancake breakfast. How many men would have bothered? She stopped in the middle of the room and listened as the voices and laughter of her family grew fainter and fainter in the distance, then disappeared, leaving only a chilling silence.

As David and the twins walked slowly along the sidewalk in the increasing heat, David once again sang a country and western song.

"So gross," Molly said, rolling her eyes. "No one listens to C and W, Dad."

"*I* do," he said cheerfully.

"Well, no one young does," Molly said.

David hooted with laughter. "There you go. At

thirty-two, my sweet, I have one foot in the grave. Humor the old man and let me enjoy my choice of music before I check out." He paused. "Hey, I want to stop at the store for a second and make sure all is well."

"Great," Michael said. "Can I get some gum?"

"Sure, if you pay for it," David said, glancing down at his son.

"That is such a lame rule," Michael said. "We own a store and I can't even have a free pack of gum or a candy bar or a…"

"Zip it," David said. "We've been over this tale of woe more times than I care to count. You want it, you buy it, end of story."

"Lame," Michael said.

"Dad," Molly said, "my friend Angela got pink braces on her teeth. Those little metal things they stick on there are pink. Really. Can I have pink braces since I'm being forced to go through this torture?"

"We'll see."

"Mmm. I hate *we'll see* because it always seems to end up being *no.*"

"Well, sugar lump, it all depends on whether the pink ones cost more than the regular ones," David said. "We'll investigate the situation. I promise. Okay?"

"I guess." Molly sighed. "I wish we were rich."

"Money can't buy happiness," David said.

"Are you happy even though we're not rich?" Molly said.

"Yep."

"How come?"

"Easy question," David said, as they approached the area behind the store. "I'm married to your mother and we have two rather weird but fantastic kids."

"We're not weird," Michael said, laughing.

"Can we vote on that?" David said.

The trio was smiling as they entered the store through the back entrance. David swept his gaze over the interior and nodded in approval while inhaling the tantalizing aromas of fresh bread and spices that wafted through the air. Hanging plants and a cobblestone floor created the atmosphere of an inviting outdoor market. Attractive arrangements of the multitude of offerings beckoned.

Sandra did all this, David thought, for the umpteenth time. She'd turned an ordinary convenience store into a charming and unique establishment. She was really something, his lovely Sandra.

"Hey, Henry," David called out. "How's it going?"

"Busy," the young man behind the counter said. "Big run on bread, cheese and wine all morning."

"People know your mom bakes the best bread in the North End," David said, coming to the front of the counter.

"Yep," Henry said. "So, Molly and Michael, what kind of trouble are you up to today?"

"We're going swimming," Michael said. "We don't

have air-conditioning at home and it's hot. You're lucky it's your turn to work in here where it's cool."

Henry laughed. "I know. Now if the customers would quit coming in and disturbing me I could get my studying done. I'm never going to be a famous lawyer if I don't pass these courses I'm taking."

David smiled and wandered around the store as the twins chatted with Henry.

He was so lucky to have connected with the Capelli family, he mused. They were a big Italian bunch who took turns working at the store as their busy schedules allowed. Maria Capelli, the mother of the clan, provided fresh baked bread and Italian pastries, which flew off the shelves. There were some customers who only came when a Capelli was on duty because they could converse in Italian instead of faltering English.

Maria Capelli had named each of her seven children after a famous American, to the amusement of her laid-back husband, Carlo. Henry was actually Henry Ford Capelli, a fact that made the handsome young man roll his eyes in mock dismay.

David stopped at the far wall of the store where fresh produce was attractively displayed. He envisioned that wall torn down and the emporium stretching across the empty, attached building next door.

Man, he thought, talk about going into debt. But if they didn't run the risk and go for it, they'd never make more than they were now and… But could they even get a bank to loan them what it would take to… The monthly payments on that loan would be out of sight. Scary, very scary. But Sandra kept bringing up the subject of air-conditioning, making it clear she was tired of the hot apartment and…

Hell, he thought, hooking a hand over the back of his neck. He'd been chasing these kinds of thoughts around in his mind for weeks, driving himself crazy. It was definitely time to sit down with their accountant and start crunching some numbers as accountant types liked to say. Well, not today. He was going to enjoy his kids and cool off in the city pool, which would be packed with people but what the heck.

"We're outta here," David called. "Invent a new car when you finish studying, Henry Ford. We're gone."

"Yeah, yeah," Henry said, flapping a hand in the air. "Go away and stop bothering me with the car jokes. My brother Roy says you always get in a zinger about when he's going to get a horse, too."

David laughed. "Well, what do you expect when a guy is named Roy Rogers Capelli? Come on, M and M, let's go hit the waves."

When Sandra finished putting away the clean wash she made a big fruit salad, minus blueberries, for dinner and set a package of ground meat on the counter to defrost.

If David barbecued outside, she decided, she wouldn't have to turn the oven back on later and heat up the already stifling house even more. Good plan. She still needed to go to the grocery store for things that Westport's Emporium didn't carry, then maybe there would be time to finish her article on the award-winning roses blooming in Mrs. Barelli's garden.

As she added things to her shopping list she heard the distant, familiar sound of the chugging mail truck and headed down to the lobby to collect the day's offering. She retrieved the mail from the box, then walked slowly back to the elevator as she shuffled through the envelopes.

"Mmm," she said, as she entered the living room upstairs again.

A letter addressed to David from Saunders University, she mused. That was odd. He wasn't on the alumni mailing list—as only graduates were added to that multitude of people. So why were they sending something to David?

Sandra held the envelope up to the light, then tsked in disgust as her efforts did not reveal one clue as to the contents of the envelope. Darn it. Oh, well, it was probably a request for money even though David *wasn't* an official graduate.

Sandra placed the mail in its designated spot on the credenza and headed back toward the kitchen.

Her mind was once again focused on what she needed from the store, the envelope from Saunders University already forgotten.

Chapter Two

The architect who designed the apartment building where the Westports lived had been very generous in regard to the size of the platform of the fire escape accessible through the window of the master bedroom.

Three years ago four families in the building, including the Westports, had put together a plan to spruce up the platforms. The men had provided the labor in the evenings, scraping, sanding, then painting each with glossy black enamel.

The women had supplied potluck dinners and also sewed puffy cushions to sit on to hopefully catch a breeze during the tormenting summers. Kettledrum barbecues were purchased and delicious aromas wafted through the air during the spring and summer.

At ten o'clock that night David and Sandra sat on the cushions and watched the fireflies flitting through the hot and humid air. A citronella candle burned in a small holder, casting a circle of golden light.

They'd had a pleasant evening with the kids which had included the barbecued hamburgers and fruit salad for dinner, a game of Frisbee in the playground down the street, then big dishes of ice cream with a cupcake on the side before the twins headed for bed.

David yawned.

"May I quote you on that?" Sandra said, smiling over at him.

"All that sun at the pool zapped me," he said, turning his head to meet and match her smile. "But that's to be expected because our charming children informed me today that I'm old because I like country and western music."

"Well, you are in the downhill slide, sweetie pie," Sandra said. "Me? At twenty-nine I'm still in my youthful prime."

"Ah," David said, nodding. He laced his fingers on his flat stomach and closed his eyes. "Maybe I'll sleep right here tonight. It's got to be cooler outside than it is in our bedroom."

"The mosquitos obviously think so," Sandra said, smacking her arm. She paused. "David?"

"Hmm?" he said, not opening his eyes.

"Are you going to tell me what was in the letter from Saunders University?"

"What—" he yawned again "—letter?"

"The one that came in the mail today. I'd forgotten about it until now."

David opened his eyes and turned his head to frown at Sandra.

"Mail. Mail? You know, I didn't stop long enough to check the credenza. Never thought about it. There's a letter from Saunders? That's a first. I've been spared the pitch for money all these years because I'm not an alumni, per se. That's a perk of not graduating."

"Let's not broach that subject," Sandra said. "Not tonight. Aren't you curious about the letter?"

"Not curious enough to trek into the house and get it." He chuckled. "But you're obviously about to pop a seam wanting to know what it says."

"I am not," she said indignantly, then laughed in the next instant. "Yes, I am. I'll go get it. Okay?"

"Hey, you can even open it and see what the deal is."

"Nope," she said, pushing herself to her feet. "I've never opened your mail and never will. I will, however, personally deliver it to you."

"Whatever," he said, closing his eyes again.

Sandra returned minutes later and placed the letter on David's chest. She waited. Seconds ticked by.

She tapped her foot and pursed her lips. Then she picked up the letter and smacked him in the head with it. David laughed in delight and snatched the envelope from her hand.

"I wondered how long you'd last," he said, tearing the end off the envelope.

He shook out a folded piece of stationery, then tilted it toward the candlelight so he could see to read the typing.

"I'll be damned," he said finally.

Sandra sat sideways on the cushion and leaned toward him.

"What? What?" she said.

"Do you remember Professor Harrison? Gilbert Harrison?"

"Harrison," Sandra said slowly, searching her mind. "No, I... Oh, wait. Yes. He was my advisor. I saw him twice, that was it. Once to get my class list approved, and then later to have him sign my withdrawal slip when I quit. Is that who the letter is from?"

"Yeah," David said. "Here—read it yourself."

Sandra accepted the paper and shifted closer to the candle.

"He says he's planning a reunion of a select number of students and he's inviting you to come and bring your lovely wife, Sandra? He realizes that it's short notice and while it would be nice if everyone could arrive at once he realizes that might not be possible. But he does hope we'll come to the campus before the fall semester starts." She looked over at David who met her gaze. "This is strange, David. It's certainly a weird way to have a reunion. Do you think Professor Harrison has gotten senile since we were at Saunders?"

"I doubt it," David said. "He'd only…let's see…oh, probably be in his mid- to late fifties now. That's a tad young for dementia."

"I know, but this last line here where he says it's actually imperative that all those he is inviting arrive before the fall semester starts has a…a frantic tone to it, don't you think?"

"What I think is that your journalist mind is working overtime," David said. "A summer reunion just makes more sense because he'll be so busy when fall classes start up again."

"Mmm," she said. "Okay, I'll give you that one. But who are these select number of former students, and why are you one of them?"

"I don't have a clue."

"And we'll never know, because we aren't going to his planned-at-the-last-minute reunion."

"Why not?" David said, frowning. "The week after next the kids are scheduled to attend that sport camp. We'll have a whole week free. Well, we'd have to pay Henry and company to cover the store but…" He shrugged. "What the hell, it's only money."

"But…" Sandra said. " I was hoping you and I might be able to have a few days in a…a romantic bed and breakfast and…I got some brochures for you to look at and…" She sighed. "Never mind. It would be more than our budget could handle, anyway."

"Honey, listen," David said, reaching over and taking one of her hands. "The bed-and-breakfast thing sounds nice, it really does but…look, when I was at Saunders I had a lot going on with Professor Harrison. He was my advisor, I was in his freshman and sophomore English classes, and he was the batting coach for the baseball team."

"Oh," she said. "I forgot about that."

"I owe the man a lot," David continued. "He was good to me, a friend as well as all the other roles he had in my life. When I plain old flunked out he was upset *for* me, not *at* me, you get what I mean?

"My father practically disowned me because I wasn't going to be a pro baseball player, has never really forgiven me because he lived his life through me after my mom died. You know how strained things still are between my dad and me.

"Anyway, I just feel that if Professor Harrison wants me at this reunion thing, whatever it is, I should be there. Lord knows, he was always there for me when I needed him."

"I understand, David. Okay," Sandra said quietly. "I wonder how many days he wants you to be on campus? Having to go back and forth between Saunders and here is a wicked drive in the traffic. Well, whatever. Sure. It's fine."

"Hey, how about this?" he said, squeezing her hand. "I know you're disappointed about the bed-and-breakfast plan. What if we stayed in Boston in a hotel, eat out, the whole bit? I'll even go to a couple of museums with you. What do you think?"

Sandra smiled. "That sounds wonderful. Thank you, David. But I do keep wondering how long Professor Harrison expects you to be there for this reunion?"

"Even more," David said, frowning, "I wonder why the sudden reunion in the first place?"

At the church bake sale the next morning, Sandra and one of her close friends, Cindy Morrison, shuffled goodies around on the long table to make more room for the offerings. As they worked, stopping to smile at people who picked up their selections, Sandra told Cindy about the letter from Professor Harrison.

"That's not a reunion," Cindy said, shaking her head. "It's a demand—okay, I'll be nice—a *request* to a chosen group to come back to the campus. A college reunion is a whole slew of people that were in the same graduating class of whenever, stuff like that. I've never heard of anything like this Professor Harrison guy is asking for. If this was a movie I'd have the creeps by now."

Sandra laughed. "There's nothing sinister about it, Cindy, it's just unusual. Strange. Well, borderline weird."

Cindy sighed. "Well, all you can do is show up and find out what the scoop is. Plus, you get some delicious private time with that sexy husband of yours. The last time I suggested such a thing to Paul he said it sounded great, just be sure and call ahead to make sure the hotel I booked was near an eighteen-hole golf course. He's as romantic as a rock."

"But you love him," Sandra said, smiling.

"Yeah. He's a jerk, but he's my jerk. I may even forgive him for giving me a Crock-Pot for Christmas last year." Cindy paused. "Back to the mystery. You don't know the names of the other people Professor Harrison wants to see. Right?"

"Right."

"Darn. There might have been a clue there." Cindy tapped one fingertip against her chin. "You know, like they all played baseball and he's getting nostalgic in his old age and wants to see the team he helped coach. You know, like *A League of Their Own.*"

"Yes," Sandra said, nodding slowly. "It's probably something that simple. If he would have said *get together* instead of *reunion* I probably wouldn't have gotten into such a dither. It's just that, like you said, a reunion usually means a whole bunch of people and this is a chosen bunch of people and… We've been over all this. I'll give you a full report when we get back."

"Including details about your private time with sexy David?" Cindy said, wiggling her eyebrows.

"No!"

"Mom," Michael said, coming to the front of the table carrying a plate. "Can we buy these?"

"Michael," Sandra said, "I made those cupcakes. There are still some left at home."

"Not many and they're good."

"Well, thank you, sir," she said, laughing, "but go pick something someone else baked so we can have a surprise."

"What if it's gross?"

"Then we'll all die of food poisoning, or some dread disease," she said. "Live wild, Michael."

"Lame," he said, stomping away.

"He's so cute," Cindy said.

"Easy for you to say," Sandra said, "your bundle of joy is still in diapers and can't talk. Ten is a gruesome age. To Michael, everything is lame. Molly? Her word for the year is 'boring,' which even includes breakfast, I'll have you know."

"Actually," Cindy said, staring into space, "breakfast is a bit boring if you think about it."

"Not my blueberry pancakes made into animal shapes," David said, seeming to have appeared out of nowhere.

"Hi, David," Cindy said, smiling. "Sandra and I have been trying to solve the mystery of the so-called reunion, but Agatha Christies we are not. I'm going to be very disappointed if it's something as boring— to quote your daughter—as a gathering of the ancient baseball team."

"Ancient?" David said, his eyes widening. "How do you feel about country and western music, Ms. Morrison? I do believe you and Paul took line-dancing lessons last year if my memory serves. According to Molly that automatically qualifies you for Medicare."

"I used to like your kids," Cindy said, laughing, "but erase that. Jeez."

"Sandra," David said, turning to his wife, "are you ready for this? I was just talking to Clem Hunter. He and Madge are leaving for Europe next week." He jiggled some keys at eye level. "He loaned us his car for the trip to Boston. A car that has air-conditioning that actually works every time you turn it on. How about that?"

"David," Sandra said, her eyes as big as saucers, "Clem drives a Lexus. We can't borrow a Lexus and take it into city traffic. What if it gets bumped or bent or something gruesome?"

"Whoa," Cindy said. "Remember what you told your son, Sandra. Live wild. Take the Lexus."

"Amen," David said, nodding decisively. "We're

going in the Lexus. The station wagon has air that works when it's in the mood and my clunker pickup doesn't have air, or heat for that matter. Oh, by the way, I put my name on some goodies for dessert from this vast array of delicacies."

"You did?" Sandra said. "Michael is picking out something even as we speak. What did you buy?"

"Some of your cupcakes."

Cindy dissolved in a fit of laughter.

On the Friday afternoon before they left for Saunders, Sandra hired a teenage neighbor to take the twins to the city pool.

She was going to have one new dress, she decided. She couldn't remember when she'd been so self-indulgent, but by the same token she couldn't remember when she'd had David all to herself.

Whatever Professor Harrison wanted of David, it wouldn't take up his time for twenty-four hours a day. And when bedtime came it would be just the two of them in the luscious hotel where David had made the reservations.

Her first thought had been to buy a seductive nightie, but she'd shifted mental gears and decided she'd rather have a special dress to wear to one of the romantic and just-the-two-of-them dinners they would share.

As Sandra browsed through a medium-priced store, she frowned.

She was counting so much on this trip putting the spark back into her and David's marriage. She wanted him to look at her and realize he still loved her, tell her so with that love glowing in his eyes, erase from his mind the idea of leaving her when the twins were grown. She wanted him to make sweet, sweet love to her for hours, declaring his love and devotion over and over. She wanted to come home knowing they still had a forever together.

Sandra sighed as she took a hanger from a rack and held the dress at arm's length to scrutinize it.

Or was it too late for any of that? she thought miserably. Would being back on the Saunders University campus just emphasize to David how close he had come to achieving his dreams of being a professional ball player and all that status would bring to his world? Dreams that had been shattered by her tearful announcement that she was pregnant. Would this trip do more damage to their marriage than good? God, what a depressing thought.

Sandra returned home without a new dress, her enthusiasm for the purchase completely erased by her chilling thoughts. She had a long, loud cry in the shower.

Even though the incredible Lexus now sat in their driveway, Sandra put her foot down about making the trip to Connecticut in the expensive car to meet her parents, who were going to take care of the twins during their week at sport camp.

"Absolutely not, David," she said, planting her hands on her hips. "The kids think they're starving two seconds after they fasten their seat belts. I'll be a nervous wreck the whole time because I'll be afraid they'll spill something or get that butter-soft leather sticky or… No. No, no, no. We're going in the wagon."

"But…"

"No!"

David nodded. "I have a great idea. Let's drive to Connecticut in the station wagon."

"You're a wise man, Mr. Westport."

On Sunday they drove to the agreed-upon meeting place in Bridgeport, Connecticut, where they enjoyed lunch with Sandra's parents.

"This whole reunion mystery is fascinating," her mother said in the restaurant.

"Only because this Professor Harrison used the word reunion," Sandra's father said, "instead of saying he'd like to see a few of his favorite students again if possible. You women are making too much of this thing. Right, David?" He looked at his son-in-law. "Right?"

David shrugged. "I don't know. There was a…oh, a strange tone to the letter from Professor Harrison.

I should have brought the letter along so you could see what I mean. I'm afraid I'll have to side with the ladies on this one. It is a tad mysterious."

"Score one for us, darling," Sandra's mother said, patting her daughter's hand.

"Professor Harrison brainwashed you when you were going there," Michael said, in a deep voice. "You are under his control, Dad, and when he says a certain word you will be powerless. The time has come for you to carry out a secret assignment, which will result in pizza being delivered to our house three times a week free of charge for the next one hundred and fifty years. That is the mystery surrounding his demand to see you."

Molly giggled.

"I understand," David said, matching Michael's deep tone. "I have only one question, Mighty Michael."

"Speak."

"What toppings are on the pizzas?"

"May I come live with you, Mother?" Sandra said.

"No, dear. I'm afraid whatever it is those two have might be catching. You may already be affected. Have you made out your will? I'd like to have the cute little garden gnome you have on the fire escape."

"Oh, for heaven's sake," Sandra said, laughing. "This entire family is cuckoo."

* * *

When Sandra and David drove out of the parking lot to the restaurant, Sandra sniffled.

"The kids looked so little all of a sudden, David. They're awfully young to be away a whole week."

"Yeah, I know what you mean. I almost canceled the deal at the last minute and told them to get into this vehicle because we were going home." David chuckled. "Do note that you and I are the only ones who are struggling with this. The kids were all smiles."

"I realize that." Sandra sighed. "Well, at least they'll be sleeping under my parents' roof every night during the week. That makes me feel a bit better."

"And it's not as though we're just going to be hanging around a suddenly very quiet house," David said, glancing over at her. "We're off on our own adventure."

"Yes. Staying in a fancy hotel, dining instead of just eating dinner, able to concentrate on each other with no interruptions." Sandra sighed wistfully. "It will, indeed, be an adventure. A very romantic one, don't you think?"

"Oh. Oh, sure thing. You bet."

Sandra frowned. "But you were referring to the adventure of meeting with Professor Harrison. Right?"

"Well…"

"David?"

"Guilty as charged," he said, grinning at her. "But

only because the subject practically consumed the conversation at lunch."

"Mmm," Sandra said, rolling her eyes heavenward. She looked over at David again. "Did you call Professor Harrison and tell him we were coming?"

"No, I thought about doing that," David said, his attention riveted on the heavy traffic, "but when I stopped and remembered all the times we had to cancel plans because of sick kids or an emergency at the store or car trouble, and on and on, I decided to not jinx this trip. We'll just show up and surprise him."

"In our Lexus," Sandra said, poking her nose in the air. "Oh, la-di-da."

"I'm going to make a sign to put in the back window of the Lexus," David said, smiling, "that says, 'This car is borrowed so don't hit it.'" He glanced quickly at his watch. "You know, if we make decent time getting home it won't be too late for a very enjoyable activity."

Sandra's heart did a little two-step.

Like making love? she thought. In the living room. The kitchen. Anywhere they wanted to because the house was all theirs. Or maybe in the shower. Oh, heavens, how many years had it been since they'd done that?

"Oh?" she said, attempting to produce a seductive little purr in her voice that actually sounded like she needed to clear her throat.

"Yeah. I might be able to catch the last of the baseball game on the tube. A bottle of beer, a hot batch of popcorn, put my feet up and enjoy."

Sandra's shoulders slumped. "Well, fine, David, but I want you to know that if you ever give me a Crock-Pot for Christmas I won't forgive you like Cindy would."

"Huh?"

"Never mind," she said, looking out the side window. "Just drive the car and get us home. I'm going to take a long, leisurely bubble bath when we get there."

"Good for you," he said, pressing a little harder on the gas pedal. "We both have something to look forward to this evening."

Separate somethings, Sandra thought miserably. Didn't David realize that were growing further and further apart, traveling in the same direction but not intertwined? Maybe he did, but didn't care. Why would it upset him if he didn't love her anymore?

Oh, they got along fine, didn't argue, laughed, talked, made love when they weren't exhausted, moved from one day to the next with the major focus of their existence being on their children.

Sandra sighed.

But David no longer said that he loved her.

Chapter Three

David spent Monday morning at the store, then after lunch placed his and Sandra's suitcases in the trunk of the Lexus. He opened the passenger-side door and, with a deep bow and a sweep of his arm invited Sandra to enter the lush automobile. She sank onto the leather seat and laughed in delight.

"Oh, my gosh, David," she said, "this is incredible. It's like sitting on a marshmallow."

David chuckled. "Which, of course, you do all the time so you're in a position to make that comparison."

"Oh, hush. You know what I mean. I could get used to this. Forget that. I'd better not get used to this."

David closed the door and came around to slide behind the wheel. He turned the key in the ignition and the engine purred to life.

"Oh, yeah," he said. "That's it. That's all I have to say. Just…oh, yeah."

"Well, here we go," Sandra said, as David backed out of the driveway. "We're off to Saunders University where we haven't been in over ten years. I wonder if the campus has changed much?"

"I doubt it," David said, turning on the radio. "It's a landmark type place. People want it to stay the same. You know, something solid, old-fashioned looking, generation after generation with its rolling green lawns, tall shade trees, two- and three-story red brick buildings. It's sort of a postcard-perfect example of an eastern college. I think the only addition in years has been the bike racks."

"I suppose you're right," Sandra said. "They may have purchased more of the surrounding homes to convert into dorms for the students, though. There was an article in the paper last year about the student population of Saunders getting bigger every year."

"Student population," David said, smiling over at her. "Be prepared, my sweet, because I have a feeling that any of said students that we see who are attending the summer session are going to look very, very young to us. Ten years is a long time."

"Being on that campus is going to bring back a

great many memories, David," Sandra said, looking at him intently. "I'm sure you'll be remembering how close you came to achieving your dreams for your career as a professional baseball player."

"I suppose," he said, with a shrug. "But that's old news. My father is the only one still pouting and brooding about it."

"Don't you think of what could have been when you watch a professional game like you did last night?"

"Only when the announcer mentions how much money those guys make and I'm worried about paying for the twins' braces," he said, laughing.

"I still think you're going to have a rush of memories when you set foot on that campus."

David frowned. "Am I missing a message here? Are you trying to make a point that is going right over the top of my head?"

"Well, I…" Sandra sighed. "Never mind. I'll be quiet so you can concentrate on driving. The traffic is already bumper to bumper and we don't want any of those bumpers hitting this car."

"Right."

David glanced quickly at Sandra again, then redirected his attention to the sea of vehicles surrounding him.

What was going on in Sandra's pretty head? he thought. Why was she clutching her hands so tightly in her lap as though she was on the way to the dentist for a root canal? What was the big deal about old memories when returning to where a guy went to school? Everyone would have memories under the circumstances. It wasn't something to get uptight about.

Well, yeah, sure, once in a while when he was losing sleep, like now—because he was facing the decision about whether or not to go into deep debt to enlarge the emporium—he thought about the big bucks he could have made as a pro player.

But if things had gone that way, they might not have had twin babies and he couldn't imagine life without Molly and Michael. And there would be no Westport's Emporium, and he sincerely liked owning the store and the great people who came to shop there.

Life as he knew it now would not exist. He'd be away from home a great deal of the time, traveling with whatever team he played for. He'd be missing so much of the kids' lives and he'd hate that. He'd be sleeping in hotel rooms half of the year and not next to Sandra in their bed and he'd really, *really* hate that.

They'd live in an enormous house with air-conditioning, he mentally rambled on, with a deck constructed by strangers. There'd be no spending hot summer nights on the fire escape.

Yes, he'd like to be able to provide more for his family, even get Molly her pink braces, and a pro baseball contract would have made that possible.

Sandra could have nicer clothes and a car like this one, with air-conditioning that worked every time she turned it on. Yep, an air-conditioned house and cool air in the car.

But his connection with his family for the majority of every given year would be by phone and you couldn't get a hug over the phone. You couldn't make love to your wife over the phone, then lie there and watch her sleep, marveling at how beautiful she still was. And there probably wouldn't be time to make blueberry pancakes in the shape of animals.

No, when he added it all up, he was content with his life as it was...except for being broke most of the time. Sandra was working herself into a dither over how he might feel when the memories slam-dunked him when he walked across the campus of Saunders University. The might-have-beens. But she didn't have to worry about that. He was a very happy man.

David began to sing along with the country and western song playing on the radio, not realizing as he belted out the words that Sandra wasn't singing with him as she usually did.

The drive from the North End to the far west side of Boston took more than an hour due to the heavy traffic and several detours caused by road repairs. The Westports were more than ready to hand over the keys to the Lexus to the parking valet at the Paul Revere Hotel where David had made reservations. The five-story structure was one of Boston's finest hotels and was located about two miles from the Saunders University Campus.

Sandra was definitely smiling when David unlocked the door to the fifth floor room and stepped back for her to enter.

"Oh, David," she said, spinning around in the middle of the large room, "look at this. Antiques. I think the furniture in here is real antiques. It's like really being back in the days of Paul Revere."

"Nope," David said, peering into the bathroom. "I don't think ol' Paul had a hot tub."

"You're kidding," Sandra said, rushing across the room to look over David's shoulder. "You're not kidding. A hot tub. I've never been in one. Let's try it out right now."

"Patience, my sweet," David said, chuckling. He turned and pulled Sandra into his embrace. "Tonight we'll check out the hot tub when we don't have to get dressed again and go out."

"We wouldn't have to go out now if we don't want to," she said, circling his neck with her arms. "It's not like you have a set appointment with Professor Harrison. No one even knows we're here, David. We could lounge in the hot tub, make love, order dinner in from room service, make love and…"

David laughed. "You're acting like we're on our honeymoon."

"Well, what's wrong with that? We didn't get a honeymoon, remember? It's ten years late, but here we are."

David dropped a quick kiss on her lips.

"Hey, humor me, okay?" he said. "This reunion thing of Professor Harrison's is consuming my brain, probably because everyone we've told about it has made such a big deal out of it being strange, and weird and whatever. I don't think I'll be able to really relax until I know what the scoop is. I'd like to head over to the campus and see Professor Harrison now, put to rest all this silly speculation about what's going on. Okay?"

"Sure," Sandra said, producing a small smile as she stepped back out of David's arms. "No problem. The hot tub can wait. I would like to unpack, though, so our clothes aren't any more wrinkled than they probably already are."

"Your wish is my command," David said, heading toward the suitcases.

"Yeah, right," Sandra said, under her breath. "I definitely see an unromantic Christmas Crock-Pot in my future."

"What?" David said, looking back at her.

"Nothing. Nothing at all."

Before Sandra felt emotionally prepared for it to happen, she and David were walking across the

Saunders campus toward the building where Professor Harrison had had his office a decade before. A knot tightened in her stomach with each memory-filled step she took.

"Look at this place," David said, sweeping one arm through the air. "I told you it would look exactly the same. Well, the trees are taller. Man, those are big son-of-a-guns, aren't they? Hey, remember the time we were stretched out on this grass, supposedly studying, but actually concentrating on ice-cream cones we got from that vendor and the sprinklers came on to water?"

Sandra laughed. "Oh, I'd forgotten all about that. It was so funny. There must have been close to fifty of us who got soaked."

"It didn't do much for our ice-cream cones, either. Turned out the timer on the sprinklers was broken and the watering was usually done at night, but that afternoon we were taking a bath."

"What was it the campus newspaper said when they wrote about it?" Sandra said, narrowing her eyes. "Something about a surprise wet T-shirt contest held for all to enjoy free of charge, or some such thing."

"Yep," David said, wiggling his eyebrows. "And I do recall that you were one of those wearing a T-shirt that day. Oh, yeah, lookin' good."

"Hush," she said, punching him playfully on the arm.

"Perky," David whispered.

"Perky went south after I nursed twins, Mr. Westport. Perky was replaced with saggy."

"Small price to pay," David said, suddenly serious, "for how beautiful you were when you nursed our babies, Sandra. You always had such a serene, womanly smile on your face and I often wished I knew how to draw or paint or something so I could capture those moments forever."

"What a lovely thing to say," Sandra said, looking up at him, tears coming to her eyes.

David shrugged and pointed to a building just ahead.

"There it is," he said. "I hope Professor Harrison is in his office—otherwise this is going to be rather anticlimactic."

"Mmm," Sandra said.

She'd been beautiful when she'd nursed the twins? she thought incredulously. For heaven's sake, why hadn't David said something like that at the time, when she was feeling fat and frumpy and starving herself to death trying to lose the weight she gained during her pregnancy?

Before Sandra could decide if she wanted to slug David again, he pulled open the door to the building they had reached and ushered her inside. He stopped at the directory on the wall and nodded.

"Professor Harrison is on the second floor," he said, "same office as before. You'd think he would have been eligible for a bigger place by now. Some of those offices are twice the size his was."

"Maybe he doesn't like change. Some people are more comfortable with the familiar. I don't know, really, because I only spoke to the man twice in my life. You're the one who had so many different connections to him."

"Yes, I did, and I think you have a valid point," David said, nodding. "Without actually being able to give you an example, I just have a feeling that you're right, he doesn't like change." He paused. "Well, here we go. Hiking up a steep flight of stairs and waiting to see if we need oxygen when we get to the top because we're a heck of a lot older than when we used to sprint up staircases in a single bound."

"Oh, ha," Sandra said. "You're in terrific shape, and you know it. I'm the slug who will be gasping."

"Once a jock," David said, placing one hand on his heart, "always a jock."

"How profound."

At the top of the many stairs, Sandra informed David that she wasn't even winded and how about that, Mr. Jock?

"You're a fine example of womanhood," he said. "Enjoy it while you can because our children will soon be informing you that you're old like their father and…"

"David," Sandra interrupted, looking down the

hallway. "Isn't that...? Oh, I'm sure it is. Yes." She started quickly forward. "Rachel Jones? Oh, my gosh, Rachel, is that really you?"

A tall, slender woman cocked her head slightly and stared at the approaching Westports, an expression of confusion on her face. Then, as though a lightbulb suddenly turned on, a bright smile of recognition lit up her face and she hurried toward the couple.

"Sandra," Rachel said, giving her a quick hug, then repeating the gesture as she turned to David. "David. You two look fabulous. David, I swear, you haven't gained an ounce since you wore that tight sexy baseball uniform. Weren't those exciting days? I spent more time without a voice than with one from screaming my head off every time you came up to bat. Our star. Our school hero." She laughed. "And you look just as yummy today, you rotten bum."

And Rachel looked even better than she had ten years before, Sandra mused. Goodness, she was a beautiful woman and maturity just added to her uniqueness. She'd always had such lovely, café au lait toned skin, compliments of her African-American mother, she'd said, and she was now wearing her curly black hair longer, brushing the tops of her shoulders.

She was wearing jeans and a hip-length over-blouse. Just like ten years before, Rachel's clothes appeared a size too large for her, a trick she'd told

Sandra helped conceal what Rachel considered a skinny body she had no desire to put on display. Sandra's frequent declaration that women would kill for a figure like Rachel's had no affect on her mind-set.

"Yeah, those were the glory days," David was saying as Sandra tuned back in to the conversation between him and Rachel. "Saunders being the state champs in baseball two years in a row was really something. We had great teams back then."

"You're being too modest," Rachel said, then looked at Sandra. "Isn't he? He was the star of those teams. We never would have been state champs without him. Right, Sandra?"

"Absolutely," Sandra said, shifting her gaze to David.

David was glowing, she thought, feeling a chill course through her. His green eyes were sparkling, actually sparkling, and the smile on his face couldn't get any bigger. It had started already, the reminiscing, the dishing up of exciting memories of when David was the campus hero, the golden boy, with a fabulous future before him that included playing professional baseball when he graduated.

She wanted to go home. Right now. She wanted to grab David and run back to their little apartment and close the door, stay grounded in the reality of the world where they actually existed, not be here in the arena of what might have been possible for him.

"Are you here because you were invited to Professor Harrison's reunion, Rachel?" Sandra said, deciding she could at least change the subject from baseball to why the three of them were standing in that hallway.

Rachel nodded. "Yes, I got in yesterday afternoon. Oh, you'll never guess who Professor Harrison's secretary is. Jane Jackson."

"No kidding?" Sandra said. "It will be nice to see her again."

"Well, she's on vacation at the moment," Rachel said. "Professor Harrison has asked me to help him locate Jacob Weber with the hope he'll attend this shindig."

"That jerk?" David said, frowning. "Professor Harrison wants *him* to be part of this get-together?"

"Yes, he does," Rachel said. "Apparently Jacob is a fairly famous fertility specialist now. Hard to fathom, isn't it? That creepy Jacob could be a sympathetic doctor who is dedicating his life to making it possible for couples to have babies? That's not the self-centered Jacob we knew. But..." She shrugged. "Ten years is a long time. We should keep an open mind about him, I suppose."

"If he's so famous why is he hard to locate?" David said.

"Because he has clinics in this country and in Europe," Rachel said, wriggling her nose. "La-di-da. I guess in order to work uninterrupted by people hoping he'll take them on as patients or clients or whatever, none of the clinics will say if he's there but will gladly take a message and blah, blah, blah. So far, he hasn't called back. I'm trying to get fax numbers for the overseas clinics because Professor Harrison is paying for the calls and I'm running up his personal bill already."

"Speaking of the man who decided to have this rather strange...reunion...if you can actually call it that," Sandra said, "how is he? Has he changed much in ten years from the fun loving, smiling professor we knew?"

Rachel frowned and wrapped her hands around her elbows.

"He's changed a great deal," she said quietly. "It's sad, it really is."

"What do you mean?" David said, matching her frown.

"He hardly smiles at all now," Rachel said. "Did you know his wife, Mary, died eight months ago?"

"No," Sandra said. "Oh, that's awful. What happened?"

"He told me yesterday that Mary was always frail, had a heart condition, which was why they never had children," Rachel said. "She's been almost completely bedridden for several years and... Well, she died. Professor Harrison is only fifty-eight but he seems much older, sort of...defeated."

"He must miss his wife very much," Sandra said.

"Yes, but I think there's more going on that just that because…" Rachel said, then shook her head. "No, I'm not going to go there. It's probably just my imagination working overtime. Forget I said anything."

Sandra laughed. "Oh, like I'm just going to erase that enticing little tidbit."

"Ha," David said, with a hoot of laughter. "You might as well give up right now, Rachel, and spill it."

"No, not until I have a better handle on what's going on around here," Rachel said. "By the way, did you know that Professor Harrison is no longer teaching? As of a few years ago, in fact. Oh, and he quit coaching baseball right after you left here, David. He's strictly a student advisor and counselor now."

"Lucky students," David said, nodding.

"You're right," Rachel said, "because even in the short time I've been on campus I've seen that his approach to his kids hasn't changed. The summer session students are in and out of here, always welcome, even if it's just for a need to hang out somewhere if they're feeling homesick or overwhelmed, or want a place they know they can kick back and rap." She laughed. "Would you listen to me? Rap? I'm aging myself by opening my mouth. Rap now is music, not conversation."

"I repeat," David said, "lucky students."

"Yes," Rachel said, sighing, "but everything else

about our professor is different, and I know I'm sounding like a broken record but it's sad, it really is. You'll see for yourself when you meet with him."

"Is he in his office?" David said.

"Not right now," Rachel said. "He had an appointment with the president of the college board of directors. Some guy named Alex Broadstreet, who wasn't here when we were. I took the call from that Broadstreet guy. He said he wanted to see Professor Harrison immediately. It wasn't a nicely scheduled appointment, if you know what I mean. Professor Harrison was very stressed when he left here to answer the summons.

"That's why I think something is… No, erase that. I'm overreacting and I said I'd gather more data before I broached the subject of what is bothering the professor besides the death of his wife."

"But…" Sandra said.

"Forget it, Sandra," David said, smiling. "Rachel's lips are sealed."

"I can't stand this," Sandra said, rolling her eyes heavenward. "You're a mean woman, Rachel. Gorgeous, but mean."

"I just don't want to talk out of turn until I'm sure of what I'm saying, Sandra," Rachel said. "Okay?"

"No." Sandra laughed. "Okay."

"Why don't we go over to the cafeteria in the student union and get a cold drink?" Rachel said. "I want to see pictures of your family, get caught up on news. We three were such close friends and it's awful that we lost touch. You two dropped out after you got married, I left to get married and…poof…we were gone. We should never have allowed that to happen, but it's understandable, I guess. We had new, complicated and busy lives."

"Yep," David said, chuckling, "twin babies definitely give a whole new definition to busy."

"And those twins must be… Oh, heavens…ten years old?" Rachel said. "My bones are starting to creak. Shall we go get a soda? Maybe Professor Harrison will be in his office when we come back."

"Sounds good to me," David said. "Sandra?"

"Sure."

"This will be fun," Rachel said, as the trio headed toward the stairs. "The trophy case is still in the lobby of the student union. You can see all the goodies you contributed to it nearly single-handedly when you were here, David. Those state champion trophies are so huge and they keep them all shined and pretty. All the names of the players are engraved on them, as you know, so you'll be able to see proof-positive of what you did, Mr. Hero."

Dandy, Sandra thought. Now they were about to do show-and-tell during this trip down memory lane. Grim, very grim. Had David quickened his step a bit when Rachel mentioned his being able to see the trophies? Yes, he definitely had.

Oh, yes, she wanted to go home. Each time she'd asked David how long they were staying in the fancy hotel where he'd booked reservations, he'd given her a smug little smile and said it was a surprise. Said to pack plenty of clothes and just enjoy, the heck with the budget. That definitely didn't sound like they were returning to the safety of their little apartment tomorrow.

Sandra sighed as they left the building and turned in the direction of the student union.

"Is something wrong?" David said, glancing over at her.

"What?" she said. "Oh, no. It's just so hot and humid. It really hit me when we came out of the door."

"A cool drink will fix you right up," David said, walking even faster. "Let's hustle and get out of this heat."

And watch David drift even further out of her reach, Sandra thought, as he stares at the trophies engraved with his name and his shattered dreams.

Chapter Four

When Sandra, David and Rachel entered the student union they had to move around several yellow plastic tepee style signs with the message Caution Wet Floors in bold black letters blocking their way. An elderly man wearing a tan jumpsuit was busy mopping. They were unable to walk to the far wall where the trophy case stood.

"Oh, my gosh," Rachel said, "the trophy case is empty. I swear it was full of stuff late yesterday when I was in here."

The man who was mopping stopped and straightened to look at them.

"The trophies get polished this time each year," he said. "Took 'em down to the basement myself early this morning." He glanced at David, then did a double take.

"Say now, aren't you David Westport?"

"Yes, sir," David said, nodding.

"Knew it," the old man said, beaming. "I never forget the ones who helped fill that trophy case and you did more than most, boy. You surely could swing that bat. I can still hear the crowd go crazy when you hit another ball out of the park. Best baseball player we ever had here at Saunders.

"Sure was sorry when you didn't go pro 'cause I was getting ready to boast to my buddies that you were a Saunders boy and I knew ya...well, sort of knew ya. Saw you come in here a lot. Figure that gave me braggin' rights. But then you were up and gone. Shame. Darn shame. How come you didn't graduate and go pro, son?"

Oh, Lord, Sandra thought, this was a nightmare.

David laughed. "I traded in my bat and glove for diapers and teething rings." He slid one arm across Sandra's shoulders and tucked her close to his side. "We have the greatest twins in the world. A girl and a boy."

"Is that a fact?" the man said, grinning. "Well, can't fault you for that, now, can I? No, sir. Wife, kids, family, you know, are better than anything the pros might have offered you. Sure good to see you again, David. I'm going to tell my buddies I met up with the famous David Westport after all these years. Well, best get my floors done here so I can start shining up those trophies."

"Nice talking to you," David said.

As the trio went on their way across the lobby, Sandra glanced back at the old man who was busily swishing his mop across the floor.

"I wonder how many years that poor man has been doing these floors?" she said. "He looks about a hundred years old."

David chuckled. "Give or take a few years. I wouldn't feel sorry for him, though, Sandra. He's obviously content with his life, his job, and I'd bet he has a big, loving family. He understood right away that you, our twins, were more important to me than the pro contract that never came to be."

"Sure," Rachel said, laughing. "What's a million bucks or so anyway? Can you believe what pro players get these days?"

"Enough to buy air-conditioned houses and cars, and pink braces for their daughters' teeth," David said, frowning. "There's no escaping from the fact that they make big bucks."

"They make pink braces now?" Rachel said, raising her eyebrows.

"So says our Molly," David said, with a shrug.

"Both kids need braces so the pink ones are a maybe until I check out if they cost a bundle more."

"A professional athlete wouldn't be having this conversation," Sandra said, an edge to her voice. "He'd be busy writing out the checks for whatever he wanted. He wouldn't have had to trade in his equipment for diapers and teething rings. How can you be so cheerful, David, when you're surrounded by everything that's shouting at you about what you could have had?"

"Hey, whoa," David said, stopping in his tracks. "Where is all this coming from?"

"Here," Sandra said, sweeping one arm through the air. "Good old Saunders University, your path to fame and fortune."

"I took a diaper detour from the path," David said, grinning at her. "Come on, let's get a cold drink. Hey, Rachel, is the food any better in here than it was ten years ago?"

"No way," she said, laughing. "I had a hamburger last night that I think had been sitting there since the last time the three of us were in here a decade ago."

"Yum," David said.

Per usual for the summer, there were few students in the popular meeting place. The trio sat at table and David said he'd get the drinks. As he walked away, Rachel frowned at Sandra.

"Hey, girlfriend," Rachel said, "talk to me. You

were really upset back there a few minutes ago. David either didn't realize it or tried to jolly you out of your mood. What's on your mind?"

Sandra sighed. "I've been dreading coming to this campus, Rachel. Everywhere David goes he'll be reminded of what he could have had if I hadn't gotten pregnant with the twins. He had so many dreams and the potential to see them come true."

"He doesn't seem to resent not being able to play pro ball, Sandra. You can hear the pride in his voice, see it on his face when he talks about your kids and he's obviously still very much in love with you. Oh, and for the record…you didn't get pregnant by yourself."

"I know but… Never mind," Sandra said, as she felt tears starting to burn at the back of her eyes. "Let's change the subject."

"Okay," Rachel said, staring at Sandra intently. "But if you want to talk, I'll listen."

Sandra nodded, then forced a smile to appear as David returned to the table with the sodas.

"Oh, heavenly," she said, after taking several swallows of the cool liquid. "Now then, Rachel, bring us up-to-date on your news."

"Short and sweet," Rachel said, poking at the ice in her glass with the straw. "As you know, I left Saunders to get married before I graduated. He was a wonderful man and we were so happy together. However, he became very ill and died when we'd been together for five years."

"Oh, I'm so sorry," Sandra said.

"Yes, well, so it goes," Rachel said. "I'm a paralegal and I'm still struggling to pay off the medical bills. I really shouldn't have taken off work to come here for this reunion, but Professor Harrison has kept in touch with me all these years and has been very good to me. I just couldn't turn down his request to come. And that's my story."

"Bummer," David said, then patted Rachel's hand. "Sounds like you're eligible to join the Westport Penny-Pinching Club. We'll make you an honorary member."

"Well, aren't you sweet?" Rachel said, laughing. "Do I get a decoder ring, or something flashy?"

"Nope," David said. "Just the inside scoop on which grocery stores pay triple on coupons on what days."

"Sold," Rachel said. "I'm in."

"Enough," Sandra said. "We'll thoroughly depress ourselves if we go on and on about how broke we are." She paused. "Rachel, I realize you just arrived here yesterday, but do you know who else Profession Harrison invited to this reunion? Even more, do you have a clue as to why we're here?"

Rachel shook her head. "I don't know much. I haven't seen a list of who is invited or anything like that. As I told you I'm trying to track down Jacob

Weber. Professor Harrison said something about not having to search for Jane Jackson because she works for him. So, she's on the list. He also said he'd heard from Nate Williams and Kathyrn Price, who had agreed to come but I don't know when they plan to arrive. As to why he selected certain people to gather here, I really don't know, nor have I had a chance to ask him."

"Curiouser and curiouser," Sandra said, narrowing her eyes. "There is some link between all those who were invited."

"Don't go nuts, Nancy Drew," David said. "It could be nothing more than Professor Harrison picking former students that he was especially fond of."

"Nope, it's more complicated than that," Sandra said, lifting her chin. "My all-powerful woman's intuition is telling me so."

"Oh, brother, here we go," David said.

"I thoroughly agree with you, Sandra," Rachel said.

"Great. I'm outnumbered," David said. "I'm just going to drink my soda and shut up."

"I think you'd agree with us, David," Rachel said, "if you had heard Professor Harrison telling me to leave no stone unturned to find Jacob Weber. There's a... Oh, I don't know...a franticness about the professor's desire to gather these certain people together. It's much more than just a *wouldn't it be nice to see so-and-so again.*"

"Oh," David said. "Well... Okay, okay, you win. I'll concede that this whole business is a tad..."

"Weird," Sandra finished for him. "I don't remember anyone named Nate Williams, but I wasn't enrolled here that long, either. Kathryn Price? Oh, yes, who could forget her? I mean, hey, how many people do we know who became famous fashion models? She was so gorgeous. I hope she arrives while we're still here. It will be interesting to see how she looks ten years later."

"Probably still gorgeous," David said.

"Don't get gushy," Sandra said glaring at him, which caused him to burst into laughter.

"Well, we'll just have to be patient," Rachel said. "Professor Harrison will tell us what this is all about, and who is on the list of those invited in his own good time, I guess. How long are you two going to be here?"

"Good question," Sandra said. "My secretive husband won't tell me because we're really splurging on this trip and I'm supposed to just sit back and enjoy. Our kids are only going to be away at sport camp for a week but we can't possibly afford to stay that long. Right, David?"

"Nice try, my sweet," he said, grinning at her, "but no cigar. I'm not telling you how long I've booked that room at the snazzy hotel with the hot tub."

"You're mean," Sandra said.

"I think he's being very romantic," Rachel said.

"Thank you, Rachel," David said.

"Romantic?" Sandra said. "David?"

"Is that so hard to believe?" David said, leaning toward her. "On second thought, don't answer that. I think I know the answer."

Rachel laughed. "I have a feeling we're inching onto dangerous ground here. Shift gears and show me pictures of your twins."

The photographs were produced, the drinks finished, then the three strolled back toward the building where Professor Harrison had his office.

"I can't imagine there being room in Professor Harrison's cubbyhole for a secretary's desk," Sandra said.

"There isn't," Rachel said. "Jane uses an office right across the hall that's about the same size as Professor Harrison's. That's where I've been making the calls trying to find Jacob Weber. Every wall is lined with cabinets with a zillion files, one for each of the students Professor Harrison either taught or advised. There may be more of his files in the basement of the building, too, because he's been at Saunders since the Ice Age."

"You'd think that information would all be computerized in this day and age," David said.

Rachel nodded. "They recently got the funding to do that, but it will take forever to accomplish it for all the teachers on campus. Maybe they'll start with the most recent students and work backward." She shrugged. "I really don't know because I just mentioned that I was surprised that such an old-fashioned system was still being used and Professor Harrison said they were just beginning to switch everything to computers."

They entered the building and trudged up the stairs to the second floor. Halfway down the hall, Rachel stopped and moved to the far wall, then looked into the distance.

"Professor Harrison's office door is open so he must be back from that meeting," she said, to David and Sandra. "This is it, kiddies. Your turn."

"David," Sandra said, placing one hand on his arm, "I think you should meet with the professor alone the first time. You're the one he wants to see. He told you to bring me along because he couldn't very well say to stuff me in a closet at home and come by yourself. I doubt that he even remembers me, considering I only met with him twice over ten years ago."

"No way," David said. "You're my wife so you should be with me. Come on."

"But…"

"I'm going to go back into Jane's office and give you two the proper privacy with Professor Harrison," Rachel said. "Maybe you'll learn more about who's coming and why we're here. If you do, you'd better share the scoop with me."

"I'll go with you, Rachel," Sandra said.

"No," David said, taking Sandra's hand, "you won't."

"Shoo," Rachel said, flapping her hands at them. "Go. The man doesn't bite, you know. Heavens, he helped coach the baseball team you took to the state championships, David. He'll be thrilled to see you again."

And I'm the pregnant villain, Sandra thought, who brought all that to a screeching halt.

"It takes two, remember," Rachel said to Sandra, as though having read her mind. "Would you people just get in there?"

Rachel hurried down the hall and disappeared into an office on the left. Sandra and David stood exactly where they were and watched her disappear from view.

"Ready?" David said, not releasing Sandra's hand.

"No. Are you?"

"No." David shook his head. "We're being ridiculous. Professor Harrison is a very nice man, not the big bad wolf."

David started forward, having to tug on Sandra's hand to get her to move. At the open doorway to Professor Harrison's office David raised a loose fist to knock on the doorjamb, then hesitated as he stared at the man sitting behind the desk.

He's aged, David thought. A lot. His thick, dark hair that was just beginning to show silver strands was now totally gray and thinning on top. He was wearing a short-sleeve sport shirt and his once mus-cled arms were now thin. A smattering of age spots were visible on his hands.

David swept his gaze quickly over the small office.

It was exactly the same, he realized. Professor Harrison was sitting in the saggy leather chair behind his wooden, seen-better-days desk, bent over an open file. The walls were covered with overflowing book-cases and stacks of files were on the desk, as well as filling one of the faded chairs in front. He recognized the shape of the picture frame facing the professor and knew it held a photograph of his wife Mary. No, Professor Harrison definitely didn't like change.

David rapped lightly on the doorjamb.

Gilbert Harrison's head snapped up and in the next instant a wide smile broke across his face.

"David," he said, coming around the desk. "My God, you came. It's so good to see you."

As the professor approached, David's hold on Sandra's hand tightened.

Dear heaven, Professor Harrison looked seventy years old, Sandra thought incredulously. He had deep grooves on both sides of his mouth and purple smudges beneath his eyes. And he was so skinny, his shirt and slacks appearing far too large and... The death of his wife had done this to him? Oh, grief was a powerful weapon. But Rachel had hinted at something else plaguing the professor besides the mourning of his wife.

"It's good to see you, too, sir," David said, shaking hands with Gilbert but still clutching Sandra's hand with his other one. "You remember Sandra, my wife."

"Of course, my dear," Gilbert said, smiling at her. "Please. Come sit down, both of you." He turned toward his desk. "Oh. Let me clear that chair off." He picked up the stack of files, turned one way, then the other, finally placing the pile on the floor in front of a bookcase. "There. Sit, sit."

As Sandra and David settled onto the lumpy chairs, she pulled her hand free from his and wiggled her fingers that had been turning numb.

"Sorry," David mumbled, seeing what she was doing.

Professor Harrison sat behind his desk, folded his hands on the top of the open file and riveted his gaze on David.

"You look fantastic," Gilbert said. "You're as fit and trim as you were when you were here swinging a bat."

"I try to keep in shape," David said. "The older I get, the harder it is." He paused. "Sandra and I would like to express our sympathy to you, sir, about your wife. Rachel told us what happened and we're very sorry."

Gilbert shifted his attention to the framed picture on his desk, then gently stroked the glass-covered photograph with his index finger.

"It's been eight months, but I still miss Mary so very much," he said quietly. "It's difficult to go home to that empty house each night. I spend a great deal of time right here in this office to avoid walking into that godawful silence." He stared at the picture for another long moment, then shook his head slightly as though returning from a memory-filled place. "I want to thank you for making the effort to come here to Saunders as I requested."

"We're glad we were able to work it out so we could," David said, "but in all honesty we're a bit curious as to why you wanted to see me—us—after all these years. From what I understand this is not the usual type of reunion but rather a small, select group of people you've chosen to connect with again."

"That's true," Gilbert said, nodding and folding his hands again on the top of the desk.

David waited, fully expecting the professor to explain the reason behind the summons. No one spoke.

"Professor Harrison," Sandra said, unable to bear the eerie silence a second longer, "would you prefer to speak with David privately? I mean, I'd certainly understand because you really don't even know me."

"No, that won't be necessary," Gilbert said. "I would fully expect David to share anything I said to him with you, anyway, as that is how it should be between a husband and wife."

"Okay," Sandra said, nodding. "Then go right ahead, sir. Tell us why we're here."

"Jeez, Sandra," David said, "you're being a little pushy, don't you think?"

"No, I don't think," she said. "It's a reasonable question, David."

"Yes, it is," Gilbert said. "And I intend to explain everything to you, just as I will to Rachel, and the others when they arrive."

"Good," Sandra said, smiling. "We're listening."

"Not now," Gilbert said, causing Sandra to inwardly groan in frustration. "I'd like to take the two of you out to dinner tonight if that's agreeable. Do you like Italian food?"

David chuckled. "We live in the North End. We definitely like Italian food."

"Well, good," Gilbert said. "There's a nice little restaurant that Mary and I used to go to quite often. It's casual but cozy, will allow us to have the privacy we need. Would it suit you to meet me there at seven o'clock? I'll give you the address."

"Certainly," David said, getting to his feet.

"But…" Sandra said, not budging.

"I have appointments with students this afternoon, you see," Gilbert said, rising.

"No problem," David said, extending his hand to Gilbert.

Gilbert grasped David's hand with both of his.

"It's wonderful to see you, David. I just wish Mary... Well, she was very fond of you. She came to as many of your games as her health allowed." Gilbert cleared his throat, released his hold on David's hand, then wrote on a scrap of paper. "Here's the address of the restaurant."

"We'll see you there at seven," David said, turning to find a frowning Sandra still sitting in her chair. "Coming?"

"I suppose," she said, getting up slowly. "I just think we could at least be given a hint as to what this is all about."

"All in good time, my dear," Gilbert said. "Seven o'clock. Tonight."

"All right," she said, with a sigh.

"Professor Harrison," a young man said from the doorway, "I'm here for my appointment."

"So you are, Kevin," Gilbert said. "Come right in. These fine folks were just leaving. Oh, perhaps since you're on the baseball team here at Saunders, Kevin, you'd like to meet David Westport."

Kevin's eyes widened. "*The* David Westport? Oh, man, this is an honor for me, sir. You're a legend here at Saunders."

"Sir? Legend?" David said, not quite smiling. "I now feel about a hundred years old."

"Would it be too much to ask you for your autograph, sir?" Kevin said.

"My...autograph?" David said, squaring his shoulders. "Well, certainly. I'd be happy to.... My autograph?" He grinned at Sandra. "Wait until I tell the kids about this. Whoa."

"Mmm," she said, trying and failing to produce a smile.

As David wrote on the paper that Kevin produced, she once again saw that sparkle in David's eyes and the wide smile on his face.

If he were a professional ball player, she thought miserably, this would be old hat. It was only a matter of time before David realized that if he'd gone on to play in the major leagues this would have been part of his life, this fame that went along with the fortune. Oh, why couldn't Gilbert Harrison have just left them alone? This was just frosting the *if only* cake that she was certain was constantly a part of their existence.

"Thank you very much, Mr. Westport," Kevin said, beaming. "I'll be the envy of the rest of the team when I show them this."

Oh, give it a rest, kid, Sandra thought.

"We're gone," she said, striding toward the door. "Come on, David. We're going to mess up Professor Harrison's schedule. He has places to go, students to see. Yep. He's a busy man."

"Until tonight." David smiled at Gilbert, then hurried after Sandra, who made a beeline for the office across the hall where Rachel was working.

"Shut the door," Rachel said once David arrived.

David did as instructed.

"That kid just asked me for my autograph," he said. "Can you beat that? What a rush."

Rachel laughed. "Gosh, maybe I should have you sign my arm or something, and I'll never wash it again. I told you you were a campus hero, David."

"Legend," Sandra said, shaking her head. "That child over there called David a legend. Oh, he also referred to him as *sir.*"

"That blew it a bit," David said, chuckling. "Made me have visions of Medicare."

"How funny," Rachel said. "But moving right along. What did you find out about why we've been asked to come here by our professor."

"Nothing," Sandra said, slouching onto a chair.

"Well, you're a dud," Rachel said.

"He's taking us out to dinner tonight and will explain everything then," David said, sitting on the chair next to Sandra's. "He also said that a full explanation would be given to you, Rachel, and the others when they arrive."

"When he's ready to spill the beans," Rachel said.

"Oh, yes," Sandra said, "Gilbert Harrison is definitely running this show."

"Hey, he had appointments this afternoon," David said. "You're not being fair, Sandra."

"I don't feel like being fair. I've had enough of this mysterious behavior."

David laughed. "If one of the twins pouted like that you'd send them to their room."

Sandra opened her mouth to retort, then closed it again and shook her head.

"You're right," she said, finally. "I'm being bratty. I'm sorry."

"Well, shape up or I won't give you my autograph," David said.

"You," Sandra said, "are a dead man."

"Hold that thought," David said, then looked at Rachel. "I was shocked at Professor Harrison's appearance. I know he's not even sixty and he could pass for seventy. The loss of his wife has really beaten him up, I guess."

"That," Sandra said, leaning toward Rachel, "and whatever else is bothering him that you hinted at, Rachel."

"I'm still mulling that over," Rachel said. "Gathering my data and what have you."

"Nobody wants to talk to me around this place," Sandra said, getting to her feet. "I'm going back to the hotel and hit that hot tub."

"Follow that woman, David," Rachel said. "All kinds of interesting things can happen in a hot tub. Well, I mean, I read an article about it in *Cosmo*. Oh, and don't forget to report back to me tomorrow about what you find out at dinner tonight."

"I might be mulling it over," Sandra said, opening the door. "Not prepared to discuss it at that point in time."

"Okay, I had that coming," Rachel said, laughing. "But you'll have facts, while I'm dealing with what might be my imagination on this other thing."

"See ya, Rachel," David said. "This evening should be very interesting."

"The rest of this afternoon could be interesting, too, Westport," Rachel said, smiling, "if you play your cards right. Hot tub heaven."

David chuckled and followed Sandra from the office. Rachel watched them go, her smile fading as a wave of chilling loneliness swept through her.

Chapter Five

On the way back to the hotel, Sandra's rapidly deteriorating mood hit rock bottom as she replayed in her mind all the fuss that had been made over David about his glory days at Saunders and what the future could have held for him as a professional baseball player.

She was so close to tears that she didn't want David to witness that the moment they entered their room she announced she was going to try out the hot tub, she was sure there was some sport event David could watch on television and goodbye. She zoomed into the bathroom and shut the door before David could reply.

A short time later she sank into the warm, swirling water and closed her eyes as she rested her head on a special little pillow resting on the back edge of the tub.

Now this, she mused dreamily, was luxury. She could feel the tension ebbing from her body and she was going to blank her mind...somehow...and not allow one disturbing thought to intrude on her tranquility. Oh, yes, whoever had invented hot tubs deserved a pat on the head.

Several minutes passed and Sandra drifted into a lovely state of not being asleep, but not quite awake, either. Heavenly. Just...so...nice.

"Aakk," she suddenly yelled.

Her eyes flew open and her head snapped up as she felt something grab one of her knees. The abrupt motion caused her to slip under the neck-high water and come up sputtering.

"David!" she said, none too quietly. "Oh, my gosh, you scared the bejeebers out of me and...David Westport, you are naked in my hot tub."

David grinned. "There's room for two in here, isn't there?"

"Well, yes, but... You've never done anything like this before."

He shrugged. "We've never had access to a hot tub before. Think about it, Sandra. There are no nosy twins on the other side of that door wanting to know why we're in the bathroom at the same time when they're not allowed to be in the bathroom together at the same time. You said yourself that this is the honeymoon we never had. People do stuff like this on their honeymoon." He laughed. "I think. Hell, what do I know? Well, *we're* doing this on *our* honeymoon. Okay?"

A funny little noise escaped from Sandra's lips and she realized that she'd giggled. Giggled, for mercy sake, she thought incredulously. This was, without a doubt, the most romantic thing David had ever done. Either that or he didn't want to wait his turn to try out the hot tub. No, no, he was being romantic. Oh my, fancy that.

David maneuvered around, slid behind Sandra, then settled her between his legs, her back to his chest. He wrapped his arms beneath her breasts and she leaned her head on his shoulder, closing her eyes again.

"Oh, yeah," he said softly, "this is nice, really nice." He bent his head and trailed a ribbon of kisses down the side of Sandra's neck, causing her to shiver despite the warm water. "Mmm."

He shifted lower and rested his head on the pillow. The water continued to churn and swirl in a continuous soothing motion. David's arms dropped slowly from beneath Sandra's breasts to sink into the water and his breathing became deep and steady.

Sandra opened her eyes, narrowed them in the next instant and pursed her lips.

He'd fallen asleep, she fumed. Romantic as a fence post David Westport has actually fallen asleep while his naked wife was nestled against his body. Oh-h-h, no jury in the country would convict her if she murdered this man. This was a honeymoon? Oh, ha.

Sandra eased forward to the far end of the tub, turned around, then grabbed David's feet and pulled as hard as she could, causing him to be completely submerged beneath the water.

David shot upward, coughed, blinked several times, then glared at Sandra.

"What did you do that for?" he said, then smacked himself on the chest and coughed again. "Were you trying to drown me?"

"The thought occurred to me," she said, matching his expression. "You just flunked Honeymoon 101, Westport. You're a dud."

"Oh, really?" he said, a strange gleam radiating from his green eyes. "Drowning your husband on your honeymoon doesn't exactly give you an A-plus in this course, madam." He began to move slowly toward her. "You must pay for what you did."

"Now, David," Sandra said, with a nervous little laugh, "don't go nuts. I'm the mother of your children, remember?"

"I have no children," he said, raising his arms and curling his hands to imitate claws, "I'm on my honeymoon. But my demon bride tried to drown me and I am seeking my revenge."

"Oh, good Lord," Sandra said, with a burst of delighted laughter, "you've flipped your switch. I'm outta here."

She scrambled from the tub, grabbed a towel off the rack and made a beeline for the door, flinging it open. David was right behind her, dripping water as he came. She dropped the towel and raced across the room, but David caught her, sweeping her up into his arms and carrying her to the bed. He tossed her onto the soft mattress and followed her down, covering her wet body with his and capturing her lips in a searing kiss that stole her very breath.

He propped his weight on his forearms and raised his head a fraction of an inch.

"We're getting the bed wet," Sandra said, with a little puff of air.

"It'll dry. Are you sorry for what you did?"

"If I'm not? What then?"

"Then you are under my power. You are mine do with as I will."

"Do tell."

"No," he said, his voice very deep and very rumbly and very, very sexy. "I prefer to show, not tell."

His mouth melted over hers once again, and she wrapped her arms around his neck, sinking her fingertips into his thick, wet hair. Desire tightened low in their bodies, hotter, burning. Sandra wiggled. David groaned. And the kiss went on and on.

So this, Sandra thought dreamily, was a honeymoon. There was nothing in her mind but the exquisite sensations coursing through her. Nothing in her mind but David. Oh, how she loved this man. He was her other half, her soul mate, who at this moment was making her feel young and beautiful and so very special.

They had no worries or woes, no money problems, nor the incredible responsibility of raising two children to adulthood. It was just the two of them. Sandra and David, and nothing would be allowed to intrude into their private world of ecstasy.

David broke the kiss, drew a sharp ragged breath, then slanted his mouth in the opposite direction as his mouth melted over Sandra's once more.

This was his wife, he thought foggily. And they were on their honeymoon. They were young and carefree, had no kids or debts or crummy cars with temperamental air-conditioning. They had only each other and it was so damn good. He loved his Sandra with an intensity he wouldn't be able, nor would he attempt, to put into words.

David ended the kiss and shifted lower to draw

one of Sandra's breasts into his mouth, laving the nipple with his tongue, hearing the purr of womanly pleasure whisper from her throat. He moved to the other breast, then continued his journey lower, then lower still, savoring Sandra's soft, moist skin.

"Oh, David, please," Sandra said, her voice a near-sob. "I want you so much. Now, David. I love you, I love you, I love you."

And he loved her, his mind hummed. Forever and always.

He entered her welcoming body, burying himself deep within her heat, his heart racing, his passion soaring to a fever pitch. The rocking tempo began, then grew stronger, harder, earthy and real, carrying them further and further away from the bed to reach for the place they wanted, needed, had to go to. They burst upon it seconds apart, calling the name of the other, clinging tightly as they were flung into total oblivion.

They hovered there, breathing rough, hearts beating in a wild cadence. Then slowly, so slowly, they gentled and drifted back to the bed. David shifted off of Sandra, then tucked her close to his side.

"I like honeymoons," she whispered.

"And hot tubs?" he said, his voice raspy.

"Those, too."

"Yeah. Oh, yeah."

Sandra yawned. "Sleepy."

"Sated," he said, chuckling. "Let's nap."

"'Kay."

David drifted off to sleep. As Sandra started to doze, she suddenly frowned, then moved her head back so she could look at his peaceful face.

They had just made incredibly beautiful love together, she thought. Really magnificent. But... Oh, David, not once during that intimacy, not even once, had he declared his love for her. He had never said that he loved her.

Sandra slept, unaware of the tears that slid silently down her cheeks.

For the dinner with Professor Harrison, Sandra chose a flowered cotton sundress with narrow straps and a full skirt, and added comfortable white sandals. She'd shampooed her hair and brushed the natural curls until they shone, pretending they wouldn't get all kinky and weird once they emerged from the cool hotel into the humid night air.

Dressed in khaki slacks and a sans-tie green dress shirt that matched his eyes to perfection, David consulted a map he'd found in the desk drawer in their room to locate the address of the restaurant where they were to meet Gilbert Harrison.

"It's been too many years since we were here," he said, peering at the small print. "I can't remember where anything is."

"I've never heard of that restaurant," Sandra said, "but it doesn't mean it's new. We didn't exactly have the money to go out to eat back then."

David laughed. "I hate to mention this, my sweet, but we don't have the money to go out to eat *now.*" He paused, still staring at the map. "Okay, as far as I can tell, the restaurant Professor Harrison chose for this dinner meeting, or whatever you want to call it, is about four blocks from here. Do you want to drive over there or walk?"

"Walk," Sandra said decisively. "It's more romantic."

"Than riding in a Lexus?" David said, raising his eyebrows as he glanced over at her where she sat on the edge of the bed.

"Yes."

"Okay, we walk. But don't complain when your hair goes cuckoo from the humidity."

Sandra rolled her eyes heavenward. "I think you've exhausted your supply of romantic sayings, Westport."

"Hey, I'm just stating facts here. Darn it, I'll never be able to refold this map. I hate maps. Think they'll notice if I just stuff it back into the drawer?"

Sandra sighed, got to her feet and crossed the room to snatch up the map. Ten seconds later she handed the neatly folded map to David.

"You're very handy to have around," he said, smiling at her as he took the map, then put it away in the desk drawer.

"Your romantic tank is definitely riding on empty," Sandra said, picking up her purse. "Come on. We don't want to be late. But I swear, David, Professor Harrison better be ready to supply the answers to the questions we have about why we're here."

The night was, indeed, hot and humid but Sandra mentally vowed not to say one word about her hair turning her into a Shirley Temple look-alike. She was focused on the evening ahead and her determination to not leave the restaurant until Gilbert Harrison had divulged the truth about this strange reunion. She wanted facts, by gum, and she intended to get them.

As they strolled along the cobblestone walk, Sandra scrutinized the displays in the windows of the small shops they passed.

"We should get something for the twins," she said.

"We don't have twins," David said. "We're on our honeymoon, remember? I'd rather buy my new wife a present. Besides, your folks buy those kids so much junk they don't need a souvenir from us."

Sandra laughed. "You've got a point there. That would be just so not cool, to quote our darlings." She paused. "I hope they're enjoying the sport camp. Maybe we should call and find out if they're…"

"No," David interrupted. "What are you going to do if they hate the camp? Tell them they can come home early? No way. We scrimped and saved so they could attend that thing, and if they aren't having a super time I'll wring their necks."

"David, what a terrible thing to say," Sandra said, frowning.

He sighed and shrugged.

They walked in silence for another block.

"Are you getting nervous about this dinner meeting?" Sandra finally said. "You *are* a tad crabby."

"Not exactly nervous," David said, shoving his hands into the pockets of his slacks. "It's more of an edginess that's been building in me about why in the heck we're here. I want it all laid out on the table, for crying out loud." He glanced at Sandra and smiled. "Of course, the big mystery bit could very well be a product of your imagination and fueled by your buddy Cindy at home and Rachel here. This could be nothing more than Professor Harrison wanting to see some of his favorite students from the past."

"Do you really believe that?"

"No," David said, chuckling. "But then again, I may have become brainwashed by the female contingent."

"Well, we'll know soon enough," Sandra said breezily. "We've come four blocks so the restaurant must be right along here. I hope. My feet hurt. Oh, there it is." She pressed one hand on her stomach.

"Darn it, now I have butterflies in my stomach. Why am I nervous? *You're* the one Professor Harrison wants to see. I'm just along for the ride…in a Lexus."

"The only doings in *my* stomach are hunger pains," David said, laughing. "I'm a starving man."

"That's nothing new. You're always hungry."

David winked at her. "For all kinds of things, Ms. Hot Tub."

"My gosh," Sandra said, her hands flying to her cheeks, "I'm blushing. See what you did? I hope this place doesn't have bright lights because I'll be mortified. Blushing at my age. Ridiculous."

David laughed and pulled open the door to the restaurant. To Sandra's relief the atmosphere inside was dominated by candles burning in wax coated wine jugs on the tables and very dim lights on the ceiling.

David gave his name to the hostess and they were led to a table in the far corner where Professor Harrison was waiting and got to his feet to greet them.

"You found this place with no problem?" Gilbert said, once they were all seated.

"Yes," David said. "We walked from the hotel. The heat and humidity are still wicked but it was a nice enough stroll. I was hoping the temperature would drop more once the sun went over."

"It seems to have been especially humid lately," Gilbert said.

Oh, jeez, Sandra thought, they were going to talk about the weather? No. No way. Her nerves couldn't take anymore of this.

"Yes, very humid," she said. "However, I think we should—"

"Order dinner," Gilbert interrupted, as a waitress appeared at the table. "Just give us a minute to look at these menus."

"Sure thing," the young girl said. "I'll be right back."

"Everything is excellent here," Gilbert said. "Mary and I enjoyed many meals in this little place. I believe I'll have the lasagna."

"Me, too," Sandra said, snapping the menu closed. "David?"

"Well, I don't know," he said. "Everything sure sounds great. Do I want lasagna or spaghetti with meat and mushroom sauce? Or maybe…"

"David," Sandra said, through clenched teeth. "Pick one."

The waitress reappeared with a basket of fragrant breadsticks and David chose the spaghetti. Gilbert ordered a bottle of red wine and urged the Westports to try the bread, saying it was made fresh daily there in the restaurant. Sandra plunked a bread stick on her side plate.

"Professor Harrison," she said, "I don't mean to be rude, sir, I really don't, but could we cut to the chase? Why did you ask David to make this trip back to Saunders? And who else did you invite…for the lack of a better word?"

David dropped his chin to his chest. "Oh, man. Sandra, you're about as subtle as a sledgehammer."

"Your wife is delightful, David," Gilbert said. "And she's right. You've waited long enough to know what this is all about."

"Amen," Sandra mumbled.

"Please be patient just a few more minutes," Gilbert said, "until our meals arrive so we won't be interrupted."

"Certainly, sir," David said, sliding a glare at Sandra.

Sandra sighed and nibbled on her bread stick.

"Oh, before I forget," Gilbert said. "I had a call from the baseball coach, David. He's new since you played ball here. Anyway, he's holding some clinics on campus this summer and the players were quite excited when Kevin showed up with your autograph. The coach was wondering if you would have time to stop by tomorrow and meet those attending the clinics?"

"Oh, well, that's very flattering," David said, "but I promised Sandra I'd go to a museum with her, or wherever she wants to go so…"

"No, David," Sandra said, "that's all right. You visit the team and I'll see if Rachel is free to trek around with me."

"Are you sure?" David said.

"Yes, of course. You're a celebrity at Saunders and you earned that title. You have every right to bask in the limelight. Go for it."

"Wonderful," Gilbert said. "One o'clock tomorrow on the baseball field?"

"I'll be there," David said eagerly.

And those wide-eyed young players will ask the hero why he didn't go on to play professional ball like everyone expected him to, Sandra thought miserably. David would smile and do his usual bit about trading in the bat and ball for diapers and bottles, but the resentment within him must be building and building and...

"Plates are hot, folks," the waitress said, placing their meals in front of them. She filled the glasses with wine and left the bottle on the table. "Will there be anything else right now?"

"No, thank you, we're fine," Gilbert said.

Speak for yourself, Sandra thought, staring at her food.

"Mmm," David said, taking a bite of his dinner. "Delicious. Dig in, Sandra."

"Sure thing," she said, forcing herself to do as instructed. "Great. Really good."

Gilbert and David ate with gusto for several minutes as Sandra managed to chew and swallow three forkfuls.

"Now then," Gilbert said, "the time has come. I

can eat and talk and I promised to do just that once our dinners arrived." He took a deep breath and let it out slowly. "Please hear me out, then I'll answer whatever questions you have that I am in a position to answer."

"What does that mean?" Sandra said, frowning. "In a position to answer?"

"It will make sense once you hear what I have to say," Gilbert said. "David, I would like you to think back to when you first came to Saunders. With your high school grades being…shall we say…less than stellar…did you ever wonder why you received the scholarship you did?"

"Yes, I certainly did," David said. "I mean, sure, I played a decent game of baseball but scholarship committees supposedly look at more than just athletic ability. My grades weren't even close to what they should have been to be the recipient of what I received."

"That's true," Gilbert said, nodding. "Your scholarship was provided…was provided by an anonymous benefactor, who informed the board of directors and the administration of the university, that you were to receive it."

"What?" David and Sandra said in unison.

"Please," Gilbert said, raising one hand. "Just listen."

"But… Who…" David looked at his plate and pushed it to one side. "Yes, all right. Go on."

Sandra realized her mouth had dropped open and snapped it closed as she stared at Professor Harrison.

"You weren't the only one the benefactor provided for," Gilbert continued. "He chose the recipients of his gifts carefully and counted on me to see that things were tended to in the manner he wished them to be."

"Who is this man?" Sandra said, leaning forward. "This mysterious benefactor?"

"I said earlier," Gilbert said, "that I would answer whatever questions I am in a position to answer. I'm sorry, but I'm not at liberty to divulge the man's identity."

"Oh, this is crazy," Sandra said, sinking back in her chair. "Totally nuts."

"Calm down, sweetheart," David said, reaching over to give her hand a quick squeeze. "Professor, who else did this benefactor guy pick to receive these gifts?" He paused. "Wait a minute. Rachel. And she's trying to locate Jacob Weber. Nate Williams, Kathryn Price, Jane Jackson. Is that it? The entire list?"

"No," Gilbert said slowly, "but it isn't necessary for you know all the names."

"Okay, we'll let that go for a minute," David said. "But the bottom line is, why did you summon all of us here…now…ten years after the fact? What purpose does it serve?"

"The benefactor," Gilbert said, "wants to be

brought up-to-date on the lives of those he chose to receive the gifts. Yes, there are some he could keep track of by articles that have been written about their accomplishments in their careers.

"However, he feels that my speaking to each of you personally will give me insight as to who you have become as a person, as well. So, I'm having dinner with you this evening, and lunch with Rachel tomorrow. The benefactor also wants to know if you all used his gift well, and if you went on to pass the baton of giving."

David's shoulders slumped and he gripped the edge of the table so tightly his knuckles turned white. He stared off to the side and shook his head, before meeting Professor Harrison's gaze again.

"Well, you won't have a very shining report to deliver about me," he said, his voice flat and low. "I wasted the gift, the scholarship, because I never graduated and became a professional baseball player, which I assume was the purpose of my receiving the gift. As far as this passing the baton of giving thing? No. I haven't done that. I haven't done a damn thing for anyone. Nothing."

Chapter Six

Emotions slammed against Sandra's mind with such intensity she wrapped her hands around her elbows in an attempt to stop the chilling trembling that swept throughout her.

She wanted to throw her arms around David and comfort him, ease the pain she could hear in his voice and see on his pale face.

She wanted to rage in fury at Professor Harrison for demanding an accounting of David's life for whoever this diabolical benefactor was.

She wanted to plead with David to forgive her for being the cause of his shattered dreams.

"David, no, that's not true," she said, her voice shaking. "You mustn't say that, feel that way. You give of yourself all the time, share your natural talents by coaching Michael's little league team and Molly's soccer team.

"I've seen you leave the house to go to those practices after coming home from the store so tired you were blurry. But you were there, always there for those kids. You have passed the baton, David. You have."

"Coaching kids," David said, his voice raspy, "isn't why this benefactor person saw to it that I got the scholarship to attend Saunders. I failed to live up to the potential that the gift provided for me. Whoever he is I'm sure he'll be sorry he wasted his money on me. Coaching a few kids in the North End isn't passing the baton along, either. I had a chance because of that scholarship but…"

"I got pregnant," Sandra said, struggling against threatening tears. "That's how that sentence ends, doesn't it, David? If it hadn't been for me and the babies you would have had it all. I know you think about that, resent what happened to your dreams and… But this benefactor shouldn't make you feel guilty and ashamed because it wasn't your fault. Oh, David, I'm sorry. I'm so, so sorry."

"Sandra, my dear," Gilbert said, frowning, "and you, too, David, it was never my intention to upset the two of you so terribly. The benefactor is aware, of course, that you didn't play professional baseball, David. He's more concerned with whether you have shared your talents that were fine-tuned and increased because of the time you spent at Saunders."

"I already said he coaches the kids' teams," Sandra said, anger flashing in her eyes. "Tell the damnable benefactor to stick that in his pipe and smoke it."

"Sandra, jeez," David said, suddenly snapping back to attention. "Take it easy."

"I know you harbor resentment against me and the timing of my getting pregnant, David, but that's my cross to bear. Mine. I won't sit here quietly and have what you've done for those kids in the North End diminished."

"You make it sound as though I wish our twins had never been born," David said, "and that's not true."

"I know. I know how much you love them," Sandra said sadly. But he didn't love her, not anymore. Maybe...oh, God...maybe he never did. "It would just have been better if they would have come into our lives later, much, much later. But you *have* shared your athletic abilities and talents, passed that damn baton the benefactor is so worried about."

"Perhaps," Gilbert said gently, "there's even more David could do? Maybe for underprivileged children?"

"Well, sure," Sandra said, sarcasm ringing in her voice. "He can give up eating and sleeping and get right on that, Professor." She paused and narrowed her eyes. "Who is this benefactor? I want to know right now because I intend to give him a piece of my mind. Ten years later it comes to light that there were heavy-duty strings attached to his oh-so-wonderful gift? That stinks, it really does.

"I'm the one who pulled David from the path he was on to success. Me. David would have used that scholarship to its full potential and gone on to the pros if I hadn't gotten pregnant. Everyone knows that." A sob caught in Sandra's throat. "Everyone. Except our babies, except our beautiful babies."

"Honey, don't," David said, reaching for her hand. She snatched it away. "I think it's best if we leave now, Professor Harrison."

"Yes, of course," he said. "I'm so sorry for the upset and...so sorry."

Sandra got to her feet and headed toward the entrance of the restaurant.

"I've got to go after her," David said. "I'll think about what you said about the underprivileged kids. Okay? Tell the benefactor that I sincerely apologize for... I can hardly grasp what you said about his existence. It's so overwhelming and... Oh, man, Sandra went out the door. Good night, Professor Harrison."

"Good night, son," Gilbert said quietly.

Gilbert watched as David rushed across the room and left the restaurant.

"Oh, Mary, I didn't handle that well, not well at all," he whispered. "Oh, God, I wish you were here with me, my darling."

Outside David caught up with Sandra and fell in step beside her. He shoved his hands into the pockets of his slacks and slid a glance at her.

"Well," he said, "look at the bright side. The food was good in that restaurant. The little we ate of it, anyway."

"Not funny," Sandra said, then sniffled.

David looked up at the star-studded sky for a moment, then directed his attention back to the sidewalk.

"No, there was nothing funny about any of what happened back there," he said, sounding very weary. "I knew I didn't deserve that scholarship, but I sure snapped it up, didn't I? Greedy little bugger that I am. And now this mysterious benefactor wants an accounting of what was done with his gift. I wonder how he feels about big, fat goose eggs? Zip. Zero. Nada."

Sandra stopped and turned to face David, planting her hands on her hips.

"That's not true. Don't say that. Don't you dare say that."

David halted his step. "Coaching our own kids' teams doesn't cut it, Sandra. If anything, it's selfish. I could do a better job than the other fathers so I stepped up, hero that I am. Hell, what a joke. Any of the dads could do what I do for those kids. The baton the benefactor is centered on is still buried in ten-year-old dust."

"Who is he?" Sandra said, throwing out her hands.

"I don't know," David said, circling her shoulders with one arm and urging her forward. "But I've had enough of this for one night."

"Yes, me, too, but…David, think about this. Rachel is having lunch with Professor Harrison tomorrow. She's one of the recipients of the benefactor's gifts in some way or another and she's going to be account-able, on the hot seat, just as we were tonight. And there are the others, too, and maybe more beyond them."

"Well, some of them no doubt did great things with the start they got from the benefactor, Sandra. For all we know, I am the only one who blew it."

"Correct that," she said. "I blew it for you with two babies for the price of one."

"Hey, I contributed my share to the creation of those munchkins, remember?"

Sandra shook her head. "I don't want to discuss this any more tonight. I'm exhausted. I just want to go back to the room and get some sleep."

"What's this?" David said, wiggling his eyebrows. "On your honeymoon?"

Sandra glared at him.

"Sleep, it is," he added quickly. "Just close your gorgeous blue eyes and snore your little heart out."

* * *

Long after Sandra had gone to sleep, David sat in an easy chair and stared out the window, not really seeing what was within his view as his thoughts turned inward.

What a night, he thought, frowning. He'd known for years that he shouldn't have received the scholarship to Saunders, but it was pretty stark to hear the spoken words that it had been given to him by an outside source, some rich, eccentric guy who had named himself the benefactor.

He had enough power because of his money to force the administration of Saunders University to inform David Westport that he was recipient of a scholarship, giving the impression it had come from the university itself.

So what had the great David Westport done? He'd flunked out. He didn't get a degree. He didn't go on to play professional baseball. He didn't do one thing then, or now, to justify receiving that gift.

David shifted his gaze to the bed, the moonlight pouring over Sandra in a silvery cascade.

Man, she had been upset at the restaurant, he mused. She'd gone on and on as though she gotten pregnant with their babies all by herself, had been the sole cause of his plans for the future being derailed.

Well, she knew better, had overreacted and said things she knew weren't true. They'd created those babies together. He loved those kids and he loved his Sandra. She knew that. She'd been thrown for a loop for a bit, just as he had been, by what Professor Harrison had told them. She'd be okay after a good night's sleep.

A benefactor. Jeez. The whole spiel sounded like something out of a bad movie, but it was true. There was some weird guy out there demanding an accounting from those who had received his gifts years before.

David looked out the window again.

Pass the baton of giving. He'd flunked that, too, no matter how many times Sandra denied it. Multitudes of fathers across the country coached their kids' teams. It was no big deal, not even close, he was sure, to what the benefactor had in mind.

David yawned and got to his feet.

Well, he couldn't change the past, erase the existence of the twins, have him be a member of a professional baseball team. Nor would he want to. He'd given all that a great deal of thought already and knew he was content with his life the way it was.

But maybe, just maybe, he could do something about the future. Justify, at least a bit, being the recipient of that generous gift so many years before. Underprivileged kids, Profession Harrison had suggested. Do what with them? Teach them how to hit a baseball? Yeah, that would do a helluva lot for kids who might not know where their next meal was coming from. Not.

"Ah, Westport, that's enough for one night," he said quietly, then slipped into bed next to Sandra.

He scooted over so their heads were resting on the same pillow and inhaled the clean, flowery scent of her hair.

He needed to be close to her right now, he thought, as sleep began to claim him. She was his anchor, his other half, his true and only soul mate. God, how he loved her. And Molly and Michael? They were the best, the absolute best, even when they were being ten-year-old pains in the butt.

He'd figure out something to set things to rights about the baton thing, he thought foggily. Yeah, he would. Gotta pass…that…baton.

David slept, nestled close to the woman he loved.

The next morning neither Sandra nor David broached the subject of what had transpired at the restaurant the previous night. It wasn't far from either of their minds, but they had no desire to drag it out and deal with it again. Not yet.

They spent the morning exploring the small shops near the campus that hadn't existed when they'd been at Saunders years before. David relented on his stand of no souvenirs for the twins and bought each a Saunders baseball cap.

"I suppose you'll show them how to go through the ritual of bending the brim until they look beat-up instead of brand-new," Sandra said, laughing.

"Well, sure," David said, as they strolled along the cobblestone sidewalk. "It is so-o-o not cool to wear a baseball cap that obviously just came from the store. It has to have some character."

"Weird," Sandra said, rolling her eyes. "We could have gone to a secondhand store and gotten some with dynamite character, nearly falling apart."

"Sandra, Sandra, get with the program."

"I am. I'm thinking of writing an article about this fascinating subject for The *North End News*."

"There you go," David said. "It'll add a touch of class to that newspaper."

"In the meantime, feed me. I'm ready for lunch."

They ate at a café that offered huge, juicy hamburgers and hot, greasy fries, accompanied by milkshakes so thick they had to eat them with a spoon.

"Oh, I'm stuffed," Sandra said, with a moan. "What a piggy I am. I ate everything."

"Me, too. Sure was good," David said, patting his flat stomach. He glanced at his watch. "I'd best head for the baseball field as promised."

"Oh, Mr. Westport, sir," Sandra said, batting her eyelashes at him. "May I have your autograph?"

"No, you may not," he said sternly, "but you may have my body."

"Sold."

"What are you going to do this afternoon?" he said.

"I'm going to see if Rachel came back to that office where she's hanging out after her lunch with Professor Harrison. I just want to check, be there for her, in case she's upset or something, the way we were after hearing what the professor had to say. I wish I would have thought to ask her where she's staying so I could have warned her about the subject matter on the agenda for her private lunch with Gilbert Harrison."

"Shall we just plan to meet back at the hotel later?"

"That's fine," Sandra said.

"That's where the hot tub is."

"That's true."

"That's dynamite, Mrs. Westport."

"That's guaranteed, Mr. Westport."

Unless, she thought miserably, he totally lost track of time while surrounded by his fans on the baseball field.

When Sandra started down the hallway on the second floor of the building where Professor Harrison had his office, she immediately looked at the ceiling, realizing that no one had turned on the lights, creating a rather creepy, semidark tunnel she had to walk through. She quickened her step, hoping that

Rachel would be in the office across the hall from the professor's, with all the lights blazing.

Out of the shadows a man appeared and Sandra bumped squarely into him.

"Oh," she said. "I'm sorry. I didn't see you because the lights…" Her voice trailed off, as she looked at the man's face, not clearly visible in the dimness but yet… "Do I know you? You seem…familiar somehow. Yes, I'm sure I…"

"No," the man said gruffly, moving around her. "I've never seen you before so you can't possibly know me."

Sandra turned and frowned as she watched the man hurry toward the stairs, nearly running in his haste to leave the hallway.

Well, that was strange, she thought, turning and starting off again. That guy had acted like a thief in the night, but she couldn't think of one thing worth stealing up here. Darn it, he *had* sparked a memory, but he'd certainly been grumpily adamant about not knowing her so… Forget it. The important thing now was to see how Rachel was after her lunch with Professor Harrison.

To Sandra's relief, Professor Harrison's office door was closed and the lights were on across the hall where Rachel would hopefully be found. Sandra peered around the edge of the open doorway and saw Rachel sitting behind the desk, an elbow propped on the top of the desk, her chin resting in her hand. She was staring into space and as Sandra watched, Rachel's eyes filled with tears.

"Okay, that cooks it," Sandra said, stomping into the office.

"Oh, my gosh," Rachel said, jerking upright in her chair, "you scared me to death, Sandra."

Sandra plunked down on the chair opposite the desk. "What Professor Harrison told you at lunch blew you away, didn't it? Really upset you. Well, believe me, Rachel, the Westports' dinner with the good professor last night was no picnic, either. Oh, this makes me so mad I could just spit nails. What did Professor Harrison say to you? I presume you got the spiel about the benefactor."

Rachel nodded. "I was just so shocked to find out about this mysterious benefactor because all these years I believed the help I was receiving was coming from… Sandra, I really don't want to talk about this. I'm so sorry if that hurts your feelings but I need some time to digest all this."

"I understand," Sandra said, leaning forward. "I really do. I don't feel like rehashing everything that happened last night, either." She paused. "But, Rachel, I am determined to find out who this benefactor is. Knowing his identity isn't going to change the past, the stark facts, but I'm furious to think there's someone out there pushing our emotional buttons. That's wrong.

"To give gifts, then announce through Professor Harrison years later that there were strings attached to that so-called generosity is rotten. He must know it, too, because he is hiding in the shadows. Well, I say let's discover who he is and demand that he face us like a man."

Rachel nodded slowly. "Yes, you're right. He's hiding behind Professor Harrison, making him do the dirty work. Gilbert has so much to deal with right now that it isn't fair to him, either. Okay. Yes. We'll do it. We find out who the benefactor is and confront him." She paused and frowned. "I think we have a problem, though. How in the blue blazes are we going to find out who he is?"

Sandra sank back in her chair and stared at the ceiling, tapping one fingertip against her chin.

"Maybe," she said, narrowing her eyes, "there's something in each of our student files regarding this benefactor's gift. Well, not my file, but David's. And yours. And the others we know, so far, who have been invited to this crummy reunion."

"Maybe," Rachel said, nodding. "It's a place to start, which is better than nothing."

"Is Professor Harrison in his office?"

"No, he received another call from that creepy administrator Alex Broadstreet and had to go see him…again." Rachel sighed. "I don't want to talk about that, either, because I'm still not certain what's going on. Maybe it's nothing but… Never mind. I'm such a wreck. I hardly ate a bite of my lunch because I was so upset."

Sandra smiled. "David and I wasted delicious dinners last night, too. This benefactor person has a way of making people lose their appetites. Professor Harrison would do well to take the others he's going to drop the benefactor bomb on to a hot-dog stand so it won't break his budget when the food gets pitched."

Rachel managed to produce a wobbly smile. "Yeah."

"All right, let's gets serious here," Sandra said, rubbing her hands together. "Please don't tell me that ten-year-old student files are in the basement. There's probably spiderwebs and crawling things down there. It's spooky enough out in the hall right here without the lights on. Oh, by the way, did you see a man skulking in the shadows in the hallway?"

"Skulking?" Rachel said, laughing despite her gloomy mood. "Do people really skulk?"

"That guy definitely skulked. Did you see him?"

"No," Rachel said, shaking her head. "I was sitting here feeling sorry for myself. The building could have fallen down and I probably wouldn't have noticed."

"I thought he looked familiar somehow but…" Sandra shrugged. "It's not important. I'm so edgy that I'm overreacting to everything, I guess. Let's back up to the files."

"Well, we can start looking in these cabinets," Rachel said. "There are so many of them who knows how far back they go. But since Professor Harrison likes things the way they have always been, I imagine he has kept everything. I bet that even after the records are put on computer he'll keep his original files. Anyway, we have to begin someplace."

"You're right, so we'll start in here." Sandra smiled. "Anything to postpone the squaring off against the spiders and other creepy crawlers in the basement."

"Oh, Sandra," Rachel said, "I wish the benefactor didn't exist. It changes so much, ruins things and…" She drew a shaky breath.

"I know," Sandra said quietly. "David feels as though he didn't… Don't get me going or I'll weep buckets. Let's get to work. Whatever it takes, Rachel, we're going to find out who the benefactor is. He's not going to be allowed to hide behind Professor Harrison any longer."

Over at the baseball field, David had signed autographs as requested, realizing that he no longer felt a rush from the attention because he didn't feel he deserved to be declared a hero.

"The most important thing to remember," he said finally to the gathered group, "is your education comes first. Keep your grades up, don't run any risks of not graduating with a degree. I realize that baseball is a major part of your lives, but keep your priorities straight."

The young men nodded, hanging on every word David said. Then the coach instructed them to begin batting practice.

"I appreciate your stopping by," the coach said. "What you said was right on the mark, too. My job depends on the win and loss numbers of the Saunders team, but I still put academics first. If the grades aren't there, they don't suit up, not even my top players. My wife supports me on this, knowing full well I could get booted out of here by the board at any time that the win column doesn't satisfy them. I'm not budging on academics being number one, though."

"Good," David said, nodding, "that's good. I didn't graduate from Saunders because I just plain ole flunked out. Consequently I can't provide for my family the way I would like to. We have the basics, but any man worth his salt wants to do more than that, get the best for the people he loves. Without a college degree it can't be done. No way, no how."

"That's true, David, but there's even more to it than that."

"What do you mean?"

"These kids attending this clinic come from families financially comfortable enough that this group didn't have to work this summer to help finance their expenses here at Saunders in the fall. But what about the inner-city kid who is hanging out on the street corner, seeing no way out of the bleak existence he has?

"Sports can give young people a boost in self-esteem, make them realize there's a world beyond the one they've always known. Those street-corner kids are the ones I wish were attending this clinic." He sighed. "I'm dreaming. I wouldn't be the first coach who feels as I do and realized there wasn't a darn thing he could to change things."

"The Street Corner Crew," David said slowly. "That would look pretty sharp on the back of a baseball jersey, wouldn't it?"

"Yeah," the coach said, chuckling. "It says it perfectly. The kid puts on that shirt with no apologies about where he came from, then hits the ball out of the park just like the uptown boys. Oh, well, maybe someone, someday will... Look, I gotta get this bunch hustling. Thanks again for coming, David."

The two men shook hands, then David walked slowly across the field, deep in thought.

Chapter Seven

That night Sandra and David ate at a small café they discovered several blocks from the hotel. There were just a few selections on the menu, the food turned out to be nothing to shout about, but the prices were more in keeping with their budget.

"Anyway," Sandra said, after choking down another bite of dry meat loaf, "Rachel and I finally decided that Professor Harrison wanted to keep as many student files near him as possible rather than have them transported to the basement. So, when he ran out of room in the cabinets, he apparently began to stuff the older files in around the edges of the drawers where there was room."

"That's a unique filing system," David said, smiling.

"It's a nightmare," Sandra said, then took a tiny nibble of mashed potatoes. "We finally found your file and nearly cheered out loud."

David leaned slightly forward. "Was there anything in there, any hint, as to who the benefactor is?"

"Not that we could see," she said, her shoulders slumping. "But maybe there's a code or a memo that needs to be interpreted differently than how it reads or…I don't know. Until we find another file from someone else who is invited to the reunion we don't have anything to compare yours to."

"I suppose…well, that there's a document in there showing that I flunked out, huh?" David said, his gaze on the mountain he was building with his stiff potatoes.

"There's a withdrawal form," Sandra said quietly. "Professor Harrison signed it because he was your advisor."

"Mmm," David said, nodding. "I can sure live without seeing that thing in all its splendor." He paused. "Professor Harrison doesn't realize that you and Rachel are trying to discover who the benefactor is, does he?"

"No, he was gone all afternoon. We're going to spend more time looking tomorrow and if he sees us, he'll figure out what we're doing. If he's in a reasonable frame of mind I don't think he'll blame us for wanting to know who this mysterious benefactor is."

"I don't know, hon," David said, lifting one shoulder in a shrug. "He was pretty adamant about keeping the guy's identity a secret."

"Well, too bad," Sandra said, lifting her chin. "Rachel and I are determined to succeed."

"Go for it," David said, chuckling.

"I thought you and I could do something together in the morning, then I'll work with Rachel in the afternoon. Is that okay with you?"

"Sure," he said, nodding. "You're in your investigative reporter mode and there's no stopping you. I can entertain myself in the afternoon. What do you want to do together in the morning?"

"You pick. After all I'm leaving you high and dry in the afternoon."

"Well, my dear," David said, stroking his chin, "I have a sudden strong urge to go to a museum with you."

"Oh, you do not," Sandra said, laughing. "But it's very sweet of you to suggest that as our outing. Choose something you really want to do, David."

"Well, to be truthful I'd like to drive through the inner city of Boston. You know, the low income district with the housing projects and the kids who stand around holding up light posts on the corners."

"Whatever for?"

"I'm just thinking about some things. Could we leave it at that for now? No, never mind. I'll do that in the afternoon while I'm on my own."

"No, no, I'll go with you to that area," Sandra said quickly. "And I won't even bug you to death to tell me why we're doing it."

"What a gal," David said, grinning.

"You betcha, bud." Sandra looked at her plate and frowned. "The next time the twins are rotten we'll threaten to bring them here and make them eat meat loaf."

"I think that would fall under the heading of abuse," David said. "Let's get out of here and find a place that sells ice cream. We'll get triple scoop cones."

"That much ice cream will make me cold," Sandra said.

"In this weather?" David said, raising his eyebrows.

"Oh, yes. Chilled through and through, and the only solution for it will be a dip in the hot tub."

David got to his feet. "We're on our way. Think about what flavors you want your four scoops to be."

"Four?"

"Oh, yeah," David said, laughing. "The longer you need to be in that hot tub with yours truly the better, my sweet."

"You're wicked," Sandra said, rising.

"No, try...genius."

A short time later they had located the sought-after ice-cream shop. Sandra elected to have her four scoops in a bowl, deciding that she would never be able to keep up with the drips and dribbles caused by the hot, humid evening. David declared that he was up for the challenge and his four scoops were a mixed-flavor tower. They strolled along the sidewalk, glancing into the shop windows.

"David," Sandra said, finally, "I know that you want to surprise me with how long we're staying here but I need to tell Rachel our plans."

He nodded. "Our last night here is Thursday. This is Tuesday so that doesn't give you much time to solve the mystery of the benefactor."

"I've been thinking about that," Sandra said. "The twins are going to Bible-study day camp at the church starting next Monday and it lasts for two weeks. They have such a good time there each year. Anyway, what if I drove in here to work with Rachel on those files for a few hours each day?"

"You'd be exhausted, Sandra," David said, frowning. "That would be a wicked commute."

"I don't care about that part. I'm more concerned about the money I'd spend on gas."

"We can deal with that, I guess," David said, "but I sure don't like the idea of you making that drive everyday, especially in a wreck of a car like ours that may, or may not, have air-conditioning at any given moment."

"Don't you want to know who the benefactor is?"

David narrowed his eyes. "Yeah. Yeah, I do. Gifts

with undisclosed price tags to be paid are… I'd like to think there's a reasonable explanation for why the benefactor did it like this and the only way to find out is to confront him. Professor Harrison isn't about to divulge his identity so…"

"So I'll drive in each day and continue searching through the files with Rachel for clues."

"Well, if it appears that you're going to drop in your tracks from exhaustion the deal is off. Fair?"

"Fair."

"Oh, hell!"

"What? What?"

"My top scoop of ice cream just fell on my shoe. I was so busy talking my head off I didn't keep up with the drips. Damn."

"Gosh," Sandra said, laughing, "maybe you won't have enough ice cream left to get chilled through and you won't need to go in the hot tub."

David began to furiously lick the remaining ice cream, stopping only long enough to declare that he was close to freezing to death, which resulted in another fit of delighted laughter erupting from Sandra.

Oh, what a fun evening, she thought, as they continued to stroll. She felt so young and carefree and absolutely refused to allowed any worries or woes to intrude on her bliss. She and David were on their honeymoon, by golly, and she was hanging onto that mind-set for dear life.

Except…she couldn't help but wonder why David wanted to tour the inner city where kids spend their summer days leaning against light posts. What on earth was going through his complicated and maddeningly secretive mind?

David polished off his ice cream just as Sandra decided she couldn't eat another bite of hers, so he finished the last two inches in her bowl, as well.

"And you won't gain an ounce," Sandra said, with a cluck of disgust. She looped her arm through David's. "I never lost the last five pounds of baby fat from having the twins. Since ten years have gone by I definitely think it's here to stay…on my thighs."

"What do thighs have to do with being pregnant?" David dropped a kiss on the top of Sandra's head. "Never mind. Just know I like you just the way you are. Thunder thighs and all."

"If that was a compliment," Sandra said, laughing, "it didn't quite make the grade."

David chuckled, then sighed.

"Having that ice cream reminded me again of that time the sprinklers came on while we were indulging in cones," he said. "Man, that was a long time ago, wasn't it? We were so young and naive, just assumed that life would unfold the way we planned it. No fuss, no muss."

"That's normal for that age, I think," Sandra said, glancing at a store window.

"Now we know how quickly things can change," David continued quietly. "We go out to share a dinner with Professor Harrison and…bam…everything gets turned upside down."

"Don't push my buttons about the benefactor," Sandra said, shaking her head. "The man is a blackmailer, if you really think about it. Oh, I get so furious when I think about… No, I'm not going to ruin this nice evening by going there."

"Sandra, I… Look, I hope you understand but…"

"What, David?" she said, looking up at him as a chill swept through her that was not caused by the ice cream.

"I have to do it. I have to…pass the baton, somehow do a payback for the gift I received. Don't try to sell me again on how I'm already doing that by coaching the kids' teams because that isn't worth squat. I blew the scholarship, but it's not too late to make a difference somehow, somewhere."

"But, David, where on earth would you find the time to do whatever it is you're contemplating doing?"

"I don't know. I don't know what momentous thing I could do on my own, either. In case you haven't noticed, I don't know a heck of a lot."

"Well, one thing you should know," she said, smiling at him warmly, "is that you're *not* alone. I'll do whatever I can to help you find the peace you're seeking about this payback thing." She frowned. "Don't shut me out, David. Please. We're a team, together, we're… Are you listening to me?"

"What? Oh, sorry, my mind was off in a dozen different directions. What were you saying?"

"Never mind," Sandra said, a knot tightening in her stomach. "I guess…I guess it wasn't important."

"Hey, there's the hotel up ahead. Ready for that hot tub, ma'am."

"You bet, sir," she said, forcing a smile to appear. "Lead on, McDuff."

The next morning they drove through the inner city, the Lexus bringing stares from the teenagers standing by the light posts.

"I'm definitely not parking this baby anywhere," David said. "Man, would you look at all these kids? They've got absolutely nothing to do but hang around trying to be cool dudes. It's sad, it really is."

"They come in every nationality, size and shape," Sandra said, "including girls. It's no wonder the crime rate is so high down here. Boredom breeds mischief. I've lost count of how many of those girls have babies on their hips. Well, I shouldn't talk. I got pregnant very young myself, but still…"

"You know," David said, narrowing his eyes, "I beat myself up a lot because I feel I'm not providing enough for our kids, but our two have it pretty darn good."

"Yes, they do," Sandra said, nodding. "So do we, ol' Mom and Dad. We're not lacking for anything, David." Except ol' Dad's contentment with his life, his wife, his very existence. Oh, David. "Right?"

"Hmm? Oh, yeah, sure," David said, stopping at a red light. "Would you look at the size of that kid over there? Take a gander at his hands. I bet he could palm a basketball. I wonder if he even gets a chance to play, give it a try? Oh, check that out. Instead of a basketball, those hands just lit up a cigarette. This is depressing as hell, Sandra."

"David, the light is green."

"Oh," he said, pressing on the gas pedal.

Sandra commented on a skimpy outfit one of the girls she saw was wearing, then looked at David when he didn't reply.

Gone, she thought. She knew that look. He had turned his thoughts inward, was no longer aware that she was sitting there next to him. She couldn't reach him when he did this and there was no sense in trying.

It was as though he dropped a wall around himself that no one could penetrate, could only wait until he stepped from behind it and returned. And one of her greatest fears was that one of these days he would choose to just stay behind that wall and separate his world from hers permanently.

Without further conversation, David drove back

toward Saunders, finally asking Sandra if she wanted some lunch before she met up with Rachel.

"No, thank you," she said. "I'm still full from that huge breakfast we had. What are you going to do this afternoon, David?"

He shrugged. "I don't know. Don't worry about me. I'll be fine on my own."

I know, Sandra thought miserably. But the mere thought of going through life without David was heartbreaking to her. Big, big difference between those two mind-sets. Oh, yes, heartbreaking.

On the Saunders University campus, David got ready to drop Sandra off with her assurance that she would have no problem walking the couple miles to the hotel later.

"Good luck with the files," David said.

"I think we'll need it," she said, getting out of the car. "Bye for now."

Sandra stood on the sidewalk and watched as David merged back into the traffic and disappeared from view. With a sigh, she turned and started slowly across the campus toward the building housing Professor Harrison's office where Rachel would be waiting for her.

Halfway there she stopped and stared at a young couple in the distance who were sitting on a blanket on the lawn, laughing, talking and enjoying ice-cream cones.

That did it.

Sandra burst into tears.

It was just too much, she thought. Everything was falling apart and she couldn't cope with anymore. And there sat that couple with their ice cream, just like the day she and David had done that and the sprinklers had come on, drenching them. They'd been so young and happy, their whole lives spread out before them like a scrumptious buffet to pick and chose from.

Sandra sniffled and dug in her purse for a tissue as tears continued to stream down her face.

"No tissue?" she said, a sob catching in her throat as she peered in her purse. "No, of course not. That would mean that something had gone right. I need a tissue and I found one. But, no, I don't have a tissue and… Oh-h-h, I'm a wreck and…"

Suddenly a pristine white handkerchief appeared in front of her face, held by a masculine hand.

"You look like you could use this," a deep voice said. "Go ahead. Take it."

"I… Thank you," she said, accepting the offering and dabbing at her nose before she turned and looked up at the tall man standing behind her. Her eyes widened. "It's you, isn't it? The man I saw in the hallway when the lights were out. Right?" She blinked away her tears and cocked her head to one side. "I know you, I'm sure of it. But…"

"I have to go," the man said. "Keep the handkerchief. It's not that often that I get to help a lady in distress. But I bet things aren't really as bad as they seem to you at the moment."

The man strode away.

"Wait," Sandra said. "Who are you? What's your name? I'm sure we've met and..."

The man quickened his step, obviously having no intention of speaking with her further.

"Whatever," Sandra said, spinning around and starting off again. She used the soft linen handkerchief to wipe the tears from her cheeks. As she began to fold the handkerchief to put it in her purse she saw an initial sewn in script on one corner, the silky white thread almost invisible against the cloth. "A *W*. I swear I know you from somewhere Mr. W., no matter what you say to the contrary."

Oh, never mind, she thought wearily, stuffing the handkerchief in her purse as she entered the building where Rachel would be waiting for her. She had enough to deal with without fixating on a mysterious, skulking-in-the-shadows stranger, who she was convinced she knew but maybe not, and who had a prince-charming-to-the-rescue side to him as evidence by the handkerchief. A very expensive linen handkerchief embroidered with the letter *W* in the corner.

Boy, that really narrowed it down, she thought dryly, as she trudged up the stairs inside the building. A man who looked sort of familiar and whose last name started with W. The only place that letter would take her brain right now was directly to David Westport.

Fresh tears filled Sandra's eyes.

"Sandra, wait," a voice called.

Sandra stopped on the stairs and turned to see Rachel hurrying toward her, carrying two covered drinks in paper cups.

"I went over and got us some sodas," Rachel said, when she reached Sandra. "I hope you like… You've been crying. You're *still* crying. My goodness, what's wrong?"

"Ignore me," Sandra said, flapping one hand in the air as they continued up the stairs. "I'm in the middle of a meltdown. Or I'm having a nervous breakdown. Now there's a thought. They'll just come and cart me off to the funny farm and no one will ever see me again. Goodbye, Rachel. Goodbye, world."

They entered Rachel's office, she put the drinks on the desk, pulled two chairs close together and pointed at one.

"Sit," she said. "Talk. Before the little men in the white coats come for you, you're going to tell me what's wrong. That's what friends are for, Sandra. I'm your friend, I'm here and I'm listening."

Sandra sank onto the chair and Rachel sat opposite her, patting her on the knee.

"Come on," Rachel said. "You'll feel better if you spill it."

Gilbert Harrison came out of the office next to Rachel's which had been turned into a supply room that housed the copying machine. He flipped through the papers he had copied, then stopped dead in his tracks and frowned as he heard Sandra Westport speak in a tear-filled voice.

"David doesn't love me anymore, Rachel," Sandra said. "Maybe he never did—I don't know. I know he loves our twins, but… Oh, he puts on a good front but there's no erasing the fact if it wasn't for me he could have achieved his dreams and…

"Don't tell me I didn't get pregnant alone and ruin everything David had hoped to have. But if he'd never met me I wouldn't have gotten pregnant and… It's all come to a head, don't you see? This benefactor guy is the last straw for David. He's ridden with guilt because he wasted his gift, is determined to at least pass that damnable baton that Professor Harrison talked about."

"Well, that's good, isn't it?" Rachel said gently. "It would mean that David could get some closure, some peace of mind about the benefactor's gift."

"No, you don't understand," Sandra said, fresh tears spilling onto her pale cheeks. "David doesn't have any spare time to devote to a somehow paying back the gift. Something would have to go. That something…oh, God…is me. I just know it. I…" She shook her head, then covered her face with her hands.

Gilbert was hardly breathing as he listened to the heartrending conversation between Sandra and Rachel.

"Sandra, honey, listen to me," Rachel said. "I can't believe for one moment that David doesn't love you. You two have something special. I can see it, sense it, when you're together." She lifted Sandra's hands away from her face. "He loves you, Sandra."

She shook her head. "He never tells me that anymore. I can't remember the last time he declared his love for me, Rachel. I guess he got tired of hearing the lie floating through the air. Oh, he's good to me, isn't mean or nasty or anything, and we get along okay day-to-day but…I love him so much, Rachel. So very much, but he just doesn't love me.

"And now? Coming here to Saunders? Hearing what Professor Harrison said? It's going to blow us apart. He can't hide from the truths within himself anymore. He's going to do that baton thing and he'll have to leave me to accomplish that."

"No," Gilbert whispered, out in the hallway. "Dear God, no."

"Sandra, listen to me," Rachel said firmly. "Are you? Listening?"

Sandra retrieved the linen handkerchief from her purse, wiped the tears from her face and nodded.

"I was thrown off-kilter by what Professor Harrison told me, too," Rachel said. "I...I cried myself to sleep last night because... It's shocking news, this business about there being a benefactor involved in our lives all these years. David should be talking it through with you, telling you how he feels deep inside, but all he's saying, I guess, is that no matter what it takes he's going to do something to pay back his gift."

Sandra nodded.

"Most men are real dolts when it comes to expressing their emotions, communicating like women can. He's reacting to what Professor Harrison said and you're interpreting it wrong. I truly believe that. *David loves you.* Give him some time, some space, be patient as only women can be while he struggles with this. He's not going to leave you, sweetheart. You're his wife, his soul mate, the mother of his children. It will all work out fine, you'll see."

"I don't think so," Sandra said, pressing the handkerchief to her nose. "Oh, let's not talk about this anymore, because I'll just keep on weeping buckets and that isn't going to solve this. Nothing is. Thank you, Rachel, for being such a good friend."

"But..."

"No, enough." Sandra paused. "See this handkerchief? The man I saw in the hallway when the lights were out gave this to me outside because he saw I didn't have a tissue and the ice-cream-cone couple had made me cry and…I know that man, Rachel, but I can't put my finger on who he is. He says he doesn't know me, so I can't know him, but I swear he looks familiar…sort of. Why won't he tell me his name? Here. Look. There's a *W* embroidered on this handkerchief."

"Big clue," Rachel said, throwing up her hands. "I'm supposed to snap my fingers and say, wow, a *W*? Then your mysterious stranger must be…? You say *W* right now and I think Westport. As in David. Who should be hit upside the head for being such a…such a…man, and bottling things up inside him instead of talking to his wife. Talking to the woman he loves."

"Don't go there again," Sandra said dully. "I don't have the energy to cry anymore. I'm probably dehydrated as it is."

"Well, drink some of that soda." Rachel smiled. "Then you can cry some more if you want to."

"No, thank you," Sandra said, producing a small smile. "I already have a killer of a sinus headache from my weeping binge. Tears aren't going to fix my life. Nothing is. Well, enough of the pity party. Let's get to work."

Sandra paused. "Rachel, what are we going to tell Professor Harrison if he asks us why we're going through these files? I mean, jeez, his office is right across the hall. He's sure to notice what we're doing. I could say I'm doing research for an article I'm

planning to write for the *North End News* that I con-
tribute pieces to."

"No, we'll tell him the truth," Rachel said. "We'll
say we respect the fact that he's keeping his word to
not reveal the identity of the benefactor, but that we
are doing everything within our power to discover
who he is because we feel he shouldn't be hiding behind Gilbert Harrison. So there."

"We're actually going to say that?"

"Yep. If Professor Harrison catches us, we will.
Now, drink some soda and let's get to work."

"Okay. Oh, before I forget, Rachel, I finally got
David to tell me how long we're staying here. We're
leaving Friday morning. But my plan is to drive in
for a few hours each day and continue to help you.
The twins will be busy with Bible school day camp,
and David agreed to this as long as I don't exhaust
myself making the commute."

"David is worried about your health—you're taking on more than you should?" Rachel said, raising
her eyebrows. "Gosh and golly, doesn't that sound
like a man who loves you?"

"I'm drinking my soda now," Sandra said, shooting a glare at Rachel. "You just don't quit."

Gilbert cleared his throat loudly, waited a moment, then stepped into the open doorway of
Rachel's office, inwardly groaning when he saw the
false smiles both women produced for his benefit.

"Oh, good afternoon, ladies," he said. "How are you? Sandra, your eyes seem rather red and puffy. Are you all right?"

"Allergies," she said. "They were mowing the lawn outside and the cuttings were flying around and that stuff just gives my allergies fits."

"I see," he said. "Where's David?"

"He's…he went to a museum," Sandra said. Oh, good grief, what a stupid thing to say. "Well, no, not exactly a museum, per se, but a place that sells old baseball cards, which is kind of like a museum when you think about it. Because the cards are old. Like stuff in a museum."

"Ah," Gilbert said, nodding.

"Dumb, dumb, dumb," Rachel said, under her breath.

"Rachel," the professor said, "have you had any luck yet locating Jacob Weber?"

"Who? Oh. No, not yet. I haven't received answers to all my faxes. Maybe I should send them again."

"That might be a good idea," Gilbert said. "Well, I have work to do."

"So do we," Sandra said. "I mean, you know, catching up on each other's news after all these years. Rachel and I are just chatting like magpies."

"I'll leave you to it then," Professor Harrison said. "I do want to say, however, that if the news of the existence of the benefactor has been upsetting, which I surmise that it has, I apologize."

"It's not your fault," Sandra said. "We're not going to kill the messenger."

"That's very kind of you."

"Professor Harrison," Rachel said, "that grim administrator Alex Broadstreet hasn't bothered you today, has he?"

"Not so far," Gilbert said, sighing.

"I don't like him," Rachel said.

"Well, he's one of the new breed, Rachel," the professor said. "He feels that everything must be done by the book, no exceptions allowed. I'm more old-fashioned in some of my beliefs, I'm afraid. Now then, you two get back to catching up on your news, and you send those faxes when you have a minute to spare."

"I'll do it right now," Rachel said.

"Thank you, my dear."

Gilbert smiled, then turned and crossed the hallway to enter his office, closing the door behind him. He put the papers he was carrying on his desk, then frowned deeply as he stared at one of the far walls.

A wall that contained a combination-lock safe.

Chapter Eight

"You did what?" Sandra said, with a burst of laughter.

David was propped up against the pillows on the bed in their hotel room, his hands laced behind his head.

"I found this little hole-in-the-wall store," he said, "that had a terrific collection of old baseball cards. It was like a...a museum, you know what I mean? The guy didn't care that I couldn't afford to buy even one of the cards because they cost the earth. He seemed to enjoy having someone to talk to about the great players from the old days."

"Oh, my goodness," she said, laughing again.

David frowned. "Why is that funny?"

"Never mind," she said, waving a hand in the air. "You had to be there."

"Whatever. Bring me up to date on your afternoon. Did you find out anything about the benefactor?"

Sandra took off her shoes and crawled up on the bed to share the pillows with David.

"No," she said, sighing. "We got all excited because we found Jacob Weber's file. We spent forever comparing each piece of paper in his to the ones in yours. Zip. No clues jumped out at us with a big ah-ha, this is it."

"Maybe," David said thoughtfully, "there is only one file you need to find."

"One?"

"Yeah," David said, nodding. "Suppose Professor Harrison documented the benefactor's gifts and put all the information in one file."

"Oh. Rachel and I never thought of that. It has definite possibilities. But what if Professor Harrison kept something that important at his house where there would be no chance of anyone seeing it? We'd be doomed."

"Who knows?" David said. "All you can do is go through the cabinets in that office where Rachel is working and if nothing is there…"

"Oh, yuck, we'll have to go down to the basement where the bugs live."

"They don't eat much," David said. "Anyway, if you do all that and still don't discover the identity of the benefactor at least you two will know you gave it your very best shot." He paused. "Of course, you don't know for a fact that all the data is in one file. That's just my off-the-wall thought. Man, you and Rachel have taken on a very big and complicated project, Sandra."

"A necessary project, David."

"Hey, I'm not arguing the point. I want to know the identity of the benefactor, too. I suppose I should have been helping you guys this afternoon instead of drooling over old baseball cards."

"No, there's hardly room for Rachel and me in that office. We kept bumping into each other. There wouldn't have been space for you to work with us."

"Thank you. You just eased my guilty conscience." David yawned. "I could get used to this vacation bit. I came back here, took a little snooze, watched a baseball game on a cable channel we don't get… Ah, yes, the good life. I wouldn't move the rest of the evening except for the fact that I'm getting hungry."

"I'm *not* going to move if you say we're going back to that place with the awful meat loaf," Sandra said, snuggling closer to him.

She wanted to hold on to David so tightly, she thought, that he couldn't break free, couldn't leave her.

David chuckled, slid his hands from behind his head and wrapped one arm around Sandra.

"No way. Those potatoes could be used as brick mortar." David paused. "Damn, I can't get the benefactor out of my mind for more than five minutes at a stretch. I hate the idea that...never mind. Maybe we should see if Rachel wants to have dinner with us."

"She said she was going to grab a burger somewhere, then go see a foreign film with subtitles in English. I hate those things. I have to bob my head up and down, trying to read the stuff and watch the action so it all makes sense. Drives me nuts."

"I checked the menu for room service," David said, "with the idea that we wouldn't have to haul ourselves out of here, but the prices were out of sight so..." He sighed. "Man, I do get tired of pinching pennies. But then again, when I think about those kids we saw in the inner city this morning I tell myself to shut up. Oh, I've been meaning to ask you if you and Rachel have found out who else was invited to this grand reunion."

"No. There's no sense in asking Professor Harrison, either," Sandra said, "because he's not about to tell us."

"Did Rachel find Jacob Weber?"

"Not yet. I swear, David, we're coming up empty all the way around the block. It's very frustrating." She tilted her head back so she could look up at him.

"David, who do you think of right off the bat who has a last name that starts with W? Anyone?"

"Sure."

"Really? Who?"

"Me."

"Oh, for heaven's sake," she said, smiling. "You're no help."

"You've totally lost me."

"Never mind," she said, fiddling with a button on his shirt. "I'm probably being silly about the whole thing anyway. A lot of people can look sort of familiar but not really be someone you know. Right? Sure. But then again my instincts are screaming bloody murder that I know that man. Of course, he says he doesn't know me, so... But he keeps popping up where I am and..."

"Sandra?"

"Hmm?"

"Are you going to undo that button or just pull it off my shirt?"

"Oh. Well, I guess that depends on how hungry you are for dinner?"

"Dinner," he said, lowering his head toward hers, "can definitely wait."

Dinner was pizza consumed at ten o'clock that night.

Late the next afternoon, Sandra sighed and sank onto a chair in Rachel's office.

Nothing, she thought dismally, then glanced at her watch. And she was out of time. She had to leave within the next few minutes to head back to the hotel to meet up with David. She and Rachel were no closer to discovering who the benefactor was than when they started their snooping. Yes, sure, she'd come back next week, but at this rate…

"Phooey," she said, getting to her feet. "This is so frustrating."

Sandra looked at her watch again, hoping that Rachel would return from going to the post office for Professor Harrison in time for farewells.

As though she'd conjured Rachel up by thinking about her she came rushing into the office, causing Sandra to jerk in surprise.

"Guess who I just saw?" Rachel said, breathlessly.

"A mysterious man whose last name starts with W?" Sandra said, smiling.

"No. Kathryn Price."

"Really?" Sandra said. "Did you talk to her?"

"No, she was headed in the opposite direction from me and there's no way I could have caught up with her because a bunch of people on some kind of tour or whatever suddenly came between us."

"Darn," Sandra said. "Well, at least you saw her. Is she still as gorgeous as she was ten years ago, when she was well on her way to becoming a famous model?"

Rachel sank onto a chair and frowned. "No, San-

dra, there's something different about her. Something seems wrong with Kathryn."

Sandra pulled the other chair close to Rachel and sat.

"What do you mean?" Sandra said. "Something
different? Wrong?"

"Well, I only got a glimpse of her, but I could tell
that… She had a silky scarf over her hair and she was
clutching it beneath her chin, which I thought was a
tad strange because it's awfully hot out for any kind
of head covering like that. But just before I lost sight
of her a breeze billowed the material for a moment
and…" She shook her head.

"Rachel, what?" Sandra said, leaning toward her.

"Kathryn's face," Rachel said, frowning. "Even
though I wasn't that close to her I could tell.
Kathryn's face is scarred very badly. She's disfigured,
Sandra. Something terrible has happened to her."

"Oh, my gosh," Sandra said, straightening in her
chair. "That's awful, just so sad. It would be difficult
enough for an ordinary person to cope with, but
Kathryn was incredibly beautiful. I can't even imagine what she's been through emotionally, as well as
physically. It took a lot of courage for her to return
to Saunders like this, don't you think?"

"Oh my, yes." Rachel sighed. "Life is such a roller
coaster, isn't it? A person has everything planned,
spread out before them like a map for their future,
then…swish…everything changes."

Sandra nodded. "That's what happened to David, too. I get so confused sometimes. I want my kids to have hopes, dreams, goals as they get older, but a part of me wants to warn them not to put all their emotional eggs in that one basket because… But then again if I'm a gloom and doomer they might hold back, not go after those dreams."

"You can't protect them from…well, from life," Rachel said. "We don't have crystal balls, you know, can't see what the future holds."

"It's a good thing those crystal balls don't exist," Sandra said, "or we'd all probably just throw up our hands and quit." She paused. "Enough of this dreary stuff. I have to go meet David, Rachel, and I was hoping you'd get back here in time for me to say goodbye. I'll be back next week to continue helping with the files. I have your phone numbers here and where you're staying in case something comes up and I can't get here."

"Okay," Rachel said. "We're sure going to feel like dopes if Professor Harrison didn't keep any records at all of who received gifts from the benefactor. You know, just stored it all in his head."

"No, I can't picture that," Sandra said, shaking her head. "Time would dim the memories of the details of each person's gift, and heaven only knows how many people received things from the benefactor. I still believe there is a record of all this someplace.

And, my friend, you and I are going to find it and the identity of this person who now wants to be paid back for what he did years ago."

"So far we're getting nowhere."

"We've just begun to fight," Sandra said, getting to her feet. "Victory shall be ours…or however that saying goes. I've got to run. I'll see you next week, Rachel."

Rachel rose and the two women hugged goodbye, then Sandra hurried on her way. Rachel sank back onto the chair and frowned, her mind floating back to the moment she'd gotten the startling glimpse of Kathryn Price.

The next morning after a nearly sleepless night Gilbert Harrison hesitated, then picked up the receiver to the telephone on the kitchen wall in his house. He looked at the piece of paper where he'd written the number he wanted to call, then pressed the buttons. A few seconds later the telephone was answered on the other end halfway through the second ring.

"Paul Revere Hotel. May I help you?" a woman said.

"I… Yes," Gilbert said. "Please connect me with David Westport's room."

"One moment please."

Gilbert drew a steadying breath.

"Sir? I'm sorry but the Westports have checked out."

"You're positive of that?"

"Yes, sir."

"Well, thank you for your trouble," Gilbert said, then hung up the receiver.

He squeezed the bridge of his nose and closed his eyes as he felt a headache begin to throb painfully.

Was this a sign, he wondered, that he should back off and mind his own business? Oh, God, he just didn't know what to do. Nothing could erase from his mind the sound of Sandra Westport's tear-filled voice as she'd bared her soul to Rachel, telling her friend that David didn't love Sandra anymore, perhaps never did. How it had all come to a head because of the revealing of the truth about the benefactor, which was the last straw.

He'd listened from the shadows as Sandra said that David no longer said that he loved her, had grown tired of hearing that lie floating through the air.

By rote, Gilbert picked up his briefcase, locked the house and began the walk to the campus that he had made for so many, many years.

He didn't believe for one minute, he thought, that Sandra's fears were justified. He'd seen the way David looked at his lovely wife, seen his genuine concern for her the night she'd became so upset in the restaurant when the existence of the benefactor had been explained.

Oh, yes, David loved his Sandra.

But like so many men, himself included, Gilbert mentally continued, David had forgotten how important it was to a woman to hear that declaration of love. The male species had a tendency to think that their actions spoke for them, that flowery words were no longer necessary after a period of time since wedding vows had been exchanged.

David had no idea that his Sandra's heart was shattering into a million pieces, Gilbert thought, shaking his head. But he knew because he'd heard what Sandra had said to Rachel.

What should he do? He'd already created such turmoil in the Westports lives by telling them about the benefactor, asking what David had done to repay his gift. But he'd had no choice in the matter. The time had come for the truth of what had taken place over ten years before. His actions were being dictated by forces he couldn't control.

But he *was* in a position to soothe the fears and ease the heartache of Sandra Westport. He could sit David down and tell him what he had heard Sandra tell Rachel. But did he really have the right to interfere even further in that young couple's lives? Oh, dear God, he just didn't know what to do.

Gilbert entered the building housing his office and trudged up the stairs, feeling as though the weight of the world was on his shoulders, crushing him, making it difficult to breathe.

His existence as he knew it had begun to fall apart when he'd lost his beloved Mary, he thought, forcing one foot in front of the other. And before he could even begin to cope with her death so many other things had been flung at him like arrows piercing his very soul. His mind was a jumbled maze and he was weary, so very, very tired.

Gilbert left the stairs, walked down the hall to his office and entered, closing the door behind him. He sank onto the chair behind his desk, rested his elbows on the top of the battered piece of furniture and dropped his head into his hands, aching for the soothing, gentle touch and soft voice of his Mary.

On Sunday morning when Sandra and David pulled into traffic in the station wagon to make the trip to once again meet Sandra's parents halfway between their homes and collect the twins, David glanced over at Sandra.

"Hello, stranger," he said. "I haven't really seen much of you since we got back from our honeymoon."

"Our honeymoon," she said, smiling. "That sounds so strange after all these years. But you're right. We've been terribly busy since we got back.

"I had all our laundry to do, plus get my article for the paper written, stock the refrigerator and on and on. You've been putting in very long hours at the store to make up for the paychecks written to the Capelli crew while we were away."

"Yep."

"Ugh. Think of the loads of wash I'll be facing when I unpack the twins' suitcases. I don't even want to think about what I might find in Michael's pockets."

David frowned. "How do you really feel about all the chores at home that fall on you? Cooking, cleaning, shopping for food, playing taxi cab for the kids, all that stuff?"

"Heavens, David, I have no complaints. I enjoy my role in our family."

"Yeah, well, if we had more money you could hire a housekeeper. What you do is manual labor, Sandra. If we weren't so broke you…"

"David, stop it," she said sharply. "I know what you're doing. You're thinking about how financially set we would be if you were a professional baseball player. Just cut it out right now. We're fine just as we are. I'm beginning to think that the trip to Saunders wasn't a honeymoon, it was a nightmare. You're hung up on this payback business, too, that the benefactor is demanding."

"I don't think what he's asking for is unreasonable," he said, maneuvering through the traffic.

"I think that gifts given with strings attached that come to light ten years later is very unreasonable," she said, lifting her chin. "It puts pressure on you that isn't fair."

"Yes, it is."

"Let's change the subject before we get into an argument," Sandra said, then paused. "I keep thinking about what Rachel told me about Kathryn Price. To have something happen that leaves disfiguring scars would be a terrible trauma for the average person. Think about what it must be like for someone who was headed for a fantastic career in modeling because she was so beautiful."

"It's rough, all right," David said, nodding. "Life can sure throw some curveballs, can't it?"

Sandra laughed. "Curveballs? I think you have little baseballs chugging around in your veins instead of blood."

"Now there's an image," he said, with a hoot of laughter. "Hey, we're about to pick up two chatterbugs who spent a week at sport camp, remember? Even I might get tired of hearing about sports by the time they give us all the details."

"Never happen."

"We'll see."

They were silent for the next several miles.

"David?" Sandra said finally.

"Hmm?"

"You have realized, haven't you, that you're just not in a position to do this payback thing, this pass the baton number that the benefactor wants?"

Silence.

"David?"

"I just can't let it go that easily," he said, with a

weary sounding sigh. "I just can't. I blew the scholarship I received, Sandra, by flunking out, for Pete's sake. I have the opportunity to redeem myself here by passing the baton, or however you want to put it."

"You can't take on any more," Sandra said, her voice rising. "There just aren't enough hours in any given day. Professor Harrison will just have to explain that to the benefactor. If Mr. Moneybags, whoever he is, doesn't understand, that's just tough."

"No, I just can't buy into that theory," David said, an edge to his voice. "There has to be a way to do it. I need time to think this through, consider every possibility. Hell, I don't know. Something I'm doing now that takes up my time might have to go."

Like your wife? Sandra thought, turning her head to look out the side window. *Your marriage? Us? How's that for a plan, David? Does that work for you? Oh, dear God, David, no. Please. No.*

Sandra sniffled.

"Hey, what's the matter?" David said, glancing over at her.

"Allergies," she said, digging in her purse for a tissue. "I'll be so happy to see the kids. I really missed them."

"Yeah, me, too," David said, nodding. "I mean, sure, having a break from them was nice, but it's like they're an extension of myself, a glued on part of who I am. Without Michael and Molly I'm not David

Westport as I know him, me, whatever. I'm probably not making sense. You're the writer in the family who has a way with words, not me."

"I understand exactly what you're saying," Sandra said quietly.

Michael and Molly complete him, she thought miserably, but not once during that little dissertation did David mention her. Not once.

Sandra leaned her head back on the top of the shabby seat and closed her eyes with the intention of pretending to doze.

She couldn't talk to David anymore right now, she thought, because if she tried she'd burst into tears. And she had a knot in her stomach that said once she started crying she wouldn't be able to stop. She'd cry and cry until there were no more tears to shed and there she'd be…an empty shell with nothing left.

Chapter Nine

"Molly was awesome," Michael said, from the back seat of the station wagon. "You should have seen her, Mom, Dad. She hit that bull's-eye every time with those arrows. Wait until she shows you the blue ribbon she got."

Sandra and David exchanged quick, surprised glances.

"Well," Sandra said, "it's very nice to hear you praise your sister like that, Michael. Congratulations, Molly. I would have thought we'd have heard all this at lunch with Grandma and Grandpa."

Molly laughed. "Grandpa paid us five dollars each

not to get gushy about the camp again. He said he was on mental overload or something."

"Oh, I see," Sandra said, smiling. "No wonder we got those one syllable answers about your week while we were eating. I was beginning to think you didn't have a good time."

"No way," Michael said. "It was great. Can we go again next year?"

"We'll see," Sandra and David said in unison.

"You focused on archery, instead of soccer, Molly?" David said.

"I play soccer all the time at home, Dad, because you're the coach of our team and stuff and... I've never tried archery before and it was so cool."

"Well, that's very interesting, Molly. So, how about you, buddy?" David said. "What did you like best while Molly was discovering the world of Robin Hood, Michael?"

"Oh," Michael said, shrugging, "stuff."

"Tell him, Michael," Molly said. "He won't get mad. You won a second place ribbon and everything."

"No, forget it," Michael mumbled.

"Okay, spill it," David said, looking in the rear-view mirror at the twins for a moment then redirecting his attention to the traffic. "What am I not going to get mad about?"

"Well...um...I kinda didn't play much baseball at the camp," Michael said, staring at the toes of his shoes.

"Oh?" David said. "All right. So, what did you win your second place ribbon in?"

"Promise you won't get mad?" Michael said. "I know I'm supposed to be really into baseball but... Promise?"

"I promise," David said.

"Tell us, honey," Sandra said, shifting slightly in her seat so she could see her son.

"I won the ribbon playing...playing Ping-Pong."

David blinked, shook his head slightly, and frowned.

"What?" he said.

"See, what happened was," Michael rushed on, "it rained the first day of camp and we had to do indoor stuff. I thought it would be totally lame, but then I started messing around playing Ping-Pong and... The counselor guy said I had great hand-eye something...."

"Coordination," Sandra said.

"Yeah, that, from playing baseball and stuff. He taught me how to put a spin on the ball. Oh, man, it was awesome. They had this tournament thing? And I won second place and got a cool ribbon."

"Ping-Pong," David said.

"That's wonderful, Michael," Sandra said, reaching over and poking David in the ribs. "Isn't it, David?"

"Oh, yeah, you bet," David said. "Really...great."

"You're not mad 'cause I didn't play baseball, Dad?" Michael said. "Before we went to camp you kept telling me to remember to choke up on my bat some, not to forget that and… The counselor guy said that just because you were the coach of our little league team and just because you were a really good baseball player before you got old didn't mean I have to play baseball. Know what I mean?

"He said his father was a policeman but he sure wasn't going to be one because guns scared the bejeebers out of him. Are you mad about the Ping-Pong, Dad?"

"No, Michael," David said, smiling, "I'm not mad. I was surprised at first, that's all. You have every right to make your own choices. You, too, Molly. Just because I played some ball before I…I got old, doesn't mean it's etched in stone that you should play, Michael. You can forget about soccer, too, Molly, if that's what you want to do."

"Cool," Michael said, sighing with relief.

"I told you he wouldn't get mad," Molly said. "Hey, Dad, know what? They have archery and Ping-Pong in the Olympics. Is that awesome, or what?"

"Let's not get carried away here," David said, laughing. "The Olympics? Slow down, M and M."

"There's nothing wrong with having dreams, David," Sandra said.

David glanced over at her, then shrugged.

"Thing is," Michael said, "our school doesn't have a Ping-Pong team or anything. They don't even have a Ping-Pong table."

"No bows and arrows, either," Molly said, sighing.

"That's so lame," Michael said. "We'll probably never get to do our stuff again for as long as we live."

"Well, we could probably put together a Ping-Pong table, Michael," David said. "You know, find out what the exact measurements are, then buy some plywood, set it up on the kitchen table, then slide it under your mom's and my bed when you aren't using it. It wouldn't be tough to rig a net, either."

"Really?" Michael said. "Awesome."

"Who are you going to play against?" Sandra asked.

"My friends," Michael said, "and you and Dad, everyone who wants to try it."

"What about me?" Molly said. "What about my bow and arrows, my archery, Dad?"

"We'll think of something," David said.

"Promise?" Molly said.

"Yeah, sweetheart, I promise."

"If I can do archery somewhere," Molly said, "I won't say one more word about getting pink braces. Okay?"

David chuckled and nodded. "Sounds like a plan." He looked over at Sandra. "Well, life certainly isn't dull, is it? It's just full of surprises."

Sandra glanced quickly at the twins and saw that

they were chattering excitedly together about being able to play their newfound sports at home.

"Are you really okay about Michael not wanting to play baseball, David?" she said very quietly so the kids wouldn't hear her. "And Molly and her archery? You spent so many hours coaching her soccer team and, well, I know you pictured Michael being his father's son and what have you on the baseball diamond."

"My mistake," David said. "I just assumed that Michael would want to play ball because I did. That's as arrogant as it comes. It would be like that counselor kid's dad expecting his son to be a cop just because he was one. That father probably has more sense than I do, though. Ping-Pong. Archery. Well… whatever."

"Oh, honey, they're only ten," Sandra said. "They change their minds about things so fast sometimes it's hard to keep up. Remember when Molly wanted a totally purple wardrobe, then six months later hated the color purple? Michael might decide to play baseball when school starts just as he always has."

"No, just as I told him he would," David said. "I realize now that I never gave him a choice in the matter, didn't ask him if he wanted to play."

"Well…" Sandra stopped speaking as she realized that David was right on the mark.

"Changes," David said. "Life is full of never-ending changes. Choices. Decisions to be made."

"Yes," Sandra whispered, as a chill coursed through her. "That's how life is."

When the Westport family arrived home, the twins retrieved their award ribbons from their suitcases, then headed out the door to find their friends and tell them about the exciting time they'd had at sport camp.

David went to the store and Sandra went to the basement of the building to start the first load of many of the kids's grungy laundry. Her mother had offered to do the wash during the week, but Sandra had insisted that feeding the dynamic duo was more than enough for grandparents to take on.

Anyone looking in the windows, she mused, would come to the conclusion that things were back to normal at the Westport's after the family being away for a week.

"Not true," Sandra said aloud, as she sorted dirty clothes on the kitchen floor. "Not even close."

A mysterious benefactor had risen from the past and turned their present upside down, she thought. David was examining his life very, very closely and she was terrified whenever she dwelled on the conclusions he most likely would come to.

And just to frost the unsavory cake, Ping-Pong and archery had taken the places of baseball and soccer. Was David really accepting the fact that his son didn't want to play baseball? Or was he devastated

that Michael wouldn't follow in his father's foot-
steps with the son achieving the dreams the father
had to walk away from?

Sandra sighed, suddenly weary to the bone.

Changes, David had said, she mused. *Life is full
of never-ending changes. Choices. Decisions to be
made.* And she was filled with numbing dread about
what decisions David would make.

At the store, David asked John Kennedy Capelli
to stick around for a few more minutes before David
took over. He went next door to the attached building and peered through the window of the large,
empty expanse.

It had twice as much space as the emporium, he
thought. They could really expand, offer even more
of a variety of goods, maybe put some tables and
chairs at one end so people could sit and enjoy their
Italian pastries with one of a newly available selec-
tion of drinks right there on the spot. Yeah, there
were endless possibilities for Westport's Emporium
in this building.

Endless possibilities, he thought, hooking one
hand on the back of his neck, for all kinds of things
that had no connection whatsoever with a convenience store.

Time lost meaning as David continued to stare
through the window, his mind racing, thoughts tum-

bling one into the next in his mind so quickly he could hardly keep up with them.

"Hey, David," John Capelli called, poking his head around the corner of the emporium. "Are you going to be much longer? I've got a date tonight."

"What?" David jerked in surprise at the sudden intrusion into his jumbled mind. "Oh, sorry, John, I didn't intend to take so long over here." He started toward the store. "Big date, huh? Her name wouldn't be Jackie, would it?"

The next morning Sandra dropped the kids at church for the Bible-study day camp, the twins once again toting their award ribbons from sports camp to show their friends.

"Now behave yourself," Sandra said aloud to the ancient station wagon.

The drive to Saunders University took a full two hours due to an accident that reduced the traffic to snail-paced speed around the emergency vehicles. The air-conditioning in the car quit about halfway there and despite the fact that she was wearing cotton slacks and a sleeveless blouse, Sandra was hot and irritable by the time she arrived and finally found a place to park.

She wasn't doing anything, she decided, until she had a cool drink in an air-conditioned building.

With that resolve firmly in place she headed across

the campus to the cafeteria in the student union. In the lobby she stopped statue-still as she saw that the trophies had been cleaned and polished as promised and were once again in the glass-fronted case.

She walked slowly forward, then stopped to stare at the shining awards, David's name seeming to jump out at her from the engraved lists of the team members who had won the baseball state championships years before.

"Those were exciting times," a man said.

Sandra spun around to see Professor Harrison gazing into the trophy case.

"Yes, they were," Sandra said coolly. "David helped provide a lot of publicity for Saunders, and no doubt caused some talented athletes to take another look at this school when deciding where to attend. One would think that would be enough of a payback for the almighty benefactor."

"You're still upset," Gilbert said, with a sigh. "I'm so sorry, Sandra."

"It's not your fault," she said, her shoulders slumping. "I apologize for snapping at you, Professor Harrison." She produced a small smile. "Sure makes a person understand why a lot of messengers got killed in the past, doesn't it? There's no one else to take out frustrations on." She narrowed her eyes. "But there will be."

"Oh?"

"I'm not going to make up some…lame…to borrow my son's favorite word…story," Sandra said, "about why I'm back here on campus already. Rachel and I are determined to find out who the benefactor is and confront him, tell him just what we think of his pass the baton stuff."

"I see."

"I know you can't tell us who he is because you gave your word you wouldn't. It won't be your fault when we discover who he is. We may even enlist more help when some of the others who were invited to this nightmare reunion arrive and find out about the price tag attached to gifts they received years ago." Sandra paused. "Rachel said that Kathryn Price is here now."

"Yes, she told me," Gilbert said, nodding. "Kathryn hasn't contacted me yet, though, nor has Rachel seen her again since getting that quick glimpse of her."

"Do you have any idea what happened to Kathryn?"

Professor Harrison frowned and pursed his lips.

"Never mind," Sandra said, waving one hand in the air. "You keep secrets better than the CIA. Well, I'm going to get a cool drink, then connect with Rachel."

"How…how is David?" Gilbert said, looking at her intently.

"Troubled. Unhappy. Ridden with guilt since

hearing about the benefactor," she said sadly. "He's determined to do something to justify receiving that scholarship he feels he wasted, pay back the benefactor's gift. Our lives are never going to be the same because of what you told us. Pass that little newsflash on to the benefactor the next time you speak to him. His demands are the last straw and there's no room for it, no place to put it and…" Sandra shook her head. "I really need that soda."

"Sandra," Gilbert said, "you and David will see this situation through to its proper end together. You're a team, a united front, a couple who has been married many years and weathered whatever storms came your way. It's obvious to me that David loves you very much and…"

"Is it?" Sandra answered. "Well, Professor Harrison, just like that scholarship David received years ago, things aren't always what they seem to be. Will you excuse me, please? Rachel is going to start to wonder if I made the trip in here today."

"Yes. Yes, of course."

Gilbert watched Sandra disappear into the cafeteria, then walked slowly from the building to cross the campus to his office.

Well, he thought dismally, things hadn't changed since he'd overheard Sandra pouring out her heart to Rachel. She honestly believed that David didn't love her. That dear young woman was so unhappy and

David wasn't even aware of it. He had to do something, he really did. He had to be the messenger with grim news yet again when speaking to David Westport.

Sandra was hot, tired and frustrated when she chugged onto the street closer to dinner time than she had planned to arrive back home. She'd once again been caught in bumper-to-bumper traffic, the air conditioner forgot what its job description was, and she and Rachel had made absolutely no progress whatsoever in discovering the identity of the benefactor.

She left the elevator, trudged to the door and entered the apartment, stopping immediately as a delicious, spicy aroma reached her. She dropped her purse on a chair and hurried to the kitchen where she saw what was a Westport version of a Ping-Pong table. A piece of plywood was on the table, and clamps secured what looked suspiciously like an old tablecloth that had been called back into active duty.

"Hooray," she said, clapping her hands. "We now have a Ping-Pong table. It's looks terrific, gang."

"We just had to shellack the board so we don't get splinters," Michael said. "We got paddles and balls at the secondhand store and we're almost ready to roll. Cool, huh?"

"Way cool," Sandra said, smiling, then peered in the oven. "Speaking of ready, I think this scrumptious lasagna in the oven is calling our names."

"Okay, guys," David said, "carry the board into the bedroom while I get the dinner on the table. Then wash the paws and place bottoms on chairs. Got it?"

"Got it," Molly and Michael said in unison, carefully toting the board out of the kitchen.

"Little late, aren't you?" David said, frowning at Sandra.

"I'm sorry, David. The traffic was horrendous. Thank you for seeing to dinner."

"I was worried about you, Sandra," he said, an edge to his voice. "Did it even occur to you to pull over and give me a call, explain why you weren't here yet? Apparently not. Excuse me. I have a meal to get on to feed the family."

"Hey, wait a minute," Sandra said, grasping David's arm as he started across the room.

He stopped and looked at her, his frown still firmly in place.

"I said I was sorry," Sandra said. "I'll start out earlier tomorrow so I don't get caught in the rush-hour mess. I apologize if I worried you, but don't you think you're making too big a deal out of this?"

David glanced quickly at the doorway where the kids were already back and heading toward the table.

"We'll discuss this later," he said.

Sandra let go of his arm and planted her hands on her hips.

"Fine," she said coolly.

As delicious as the lasagna smelled and appeared, Sandra realized after taking one bite that she had lost her appetite. She managed to eat half of her serving, then carried her plate to the counter before anyone could see that she hadn't finished.

"You cooked, I'll clean up the kitchen," she said, to the front of a cupboard.

"Let's have dessert later, M and M," David said. "If we get that coating on the board tonight you'll be able to play Ping-Pong after Bible camp tomorrow."

"Cool," Michael said.

"Guess what, Mom?" Molly said. "The free space in the basement isn't big enough for me to do my archery thing."

"Why not?" Sandra said, looking over at Molly.

"Because the ribbon I won was for a distance about three times as long, you know?"

"Gosh, honey, I'm sorry," Sandra said.

"Yeah, well," Molly said, shrugging, "Michael is going to teach me how to play Ping-Pong. He needs someone to be on the other end of the table and stuff when his friends can't come over, and you and Dad are always so busy and... It's okay about the archery. They didn't even have any bows and arrows at the secondhand store anyway."

"You're being very mature about this, Molly mine," Sandra said. "It's very refreshing to have such maturity exhibited in this house," she added, shooting a dark glare at David.

"Cute," David said, pushing back his chair and getting to his feet. "Carry your plates over, then let's get back to work, double trouble. I want to take the board down to the basement to shellack it."

The three left the room and Sandra sighed as she tended to the kitchen chores.

"Isn't this going to be a fun evening?" she said, under her breath. "David is determined to have a wing-ding of an argument because I was a little late. Well, a lot late but I said I was sorry. Men are so much like…men."

When the kitchen was clean, Sandra headed for a cool shower and fresh clothes, still feeling sticky and uncomfortable from her hot drive home.

When she returned in shorts and a sleeveless blouse, the twins were on the living room floor watching television and David was sitting on the sofa reading the paper.

"Did you finish your painting?" she said brightly.

The twins nodded, obviously engrossed in the show they were watching. David turned the page of the newspaper.

"I'm going to Mars in a space ship and I'll be back in the next century," Sandra said, as she spun around and started across the room.

No one commented.

Out on the fire escape, Sandra settled onto a cushion and closed her eyes as a welcomed breeze floated over her. Several minutes passed, then she yelped in surprise and her eyes flew open when a hand splayed on her bare thigh.

"David, good grief," she said, "you scared me to death."

He sat on the other cushion, propping his elbows on his tented knees and making a steeple of his fingers.

"Were you sleeping?" he said. "Are you saying you're exhausted from the day you put in?"

Sandra folded her arms beneath her breasts.

"David, why are you doing this? You are just itching for a fight, I can tell. No, I am not exhausted. Yes, I miscalculated the time and traffic, but lesson learned. Okay? Can we put this to rest before it goes any further, please?"

David stared up at the sky for a long moment, not noticing the gorgeous sunset beginning to be painted across the heavens by nature's brush. He finally looked at Sandra again.

"I gave this whole thing a lot of thought today," he said quietly. "It suddenly doesn't make sense to me for you and Rachel to be knocking yourselves out to discover the identity of the benefactor at this point."

"At what point?" Sandra said, obviously confused.

"At the point where all you want to do is be able

to give the guy a piece of your mind for his having put a price tag on his gifts."

"That's a legitimate point," she said, her voice rising.

"Maybe. But wouldn't it be better to use your mental and physical energies to help me figure out how to pay the benefactor back, *then* find out who he is? The confrontation would then be a justification of having received the gift in the first place."

"David, no. That would be saying that what he did was fine, but what you did wasn't. But here you are, hat in hand, ready to set things to rights. No."

"Then you don't intend to help me pass the baton?"

"Oh, honey, I didn't say that," Sandra said, reaching over and grasping his hands with hers. "I don't agree with you that you have to do it, but I respect your right to feel that way and of course I'll help you.

"Please understand my position, too. The benefactor needs to be told that the way he did things was wrong, very wrong. Then, fine, inform him how you are going to pass the baton, accomplish the payback, whatever, after he realizes he should have handled things differently years ago."

David nodded slowly.

"We'll compromise on my going to Saunders, too," Sandra said. "I'll tell Rachel I can't come every day, and I will definitely leave the campus earlier so I'm home at a reasonable hour. Okay?"

David looked at Sandra intently, then freed his hands from hers and framed her face. He leaned forward and kissed her. When he broke the kiss, Sandra took a much needed breath.

"Okay," he said, smiling.

"Thank you," she said, matching his smile. "And I *am* sorry I was so late and that I worried you."

"And I'm sorry that I was such a grump about it. It just got blown out of proportion in my mind because I'd come to the conclusion that you didn't need to even be there now, then you aged me ten years by not showing up when expected and… Enough. Did you accomplish anything today?"

"Not really," Sandra said, sighing. "Oh, there was a fax from Jacob Weber just as I was leaving. I can't remember now where Rachel said it was from. England? Italy? I don't know. Anyway, he said he would arrive at Saunders per the reunion invitation as soon as possible but couldn't give an exact date at this time."

"Well, la-di-da," David said, shaking his head. "I wonder what gift Jacob the Jerk received from the benefactor?"

"Maybe he isn't a jerk anymore. I mean, he's helped countless people who have fertility problems have the babies they ached for."

"There's big money in that stuff," David said, linking his fingers on his stomach.

"You're cynical," Sandra said, laughing.

"Maybe."

"David, to completely change the subject, is Molly really okay about not being able to do her archery thing because the space in the basement is too small?"

"Yes, she is," David said, turning his head to look at Sandra. "Know why? Because M and M have decided they'll be the first brother and sister team to win Olympic Gold playing Ping-Pong. Michael is going to be Molly's coach. Oh, and they want their medals framed and hung in the living room for all to see. They claim their baseball and soccer days are over and they're concentrating solely on Ping-Pong now and forever. Preparing for the Olympics, you understand."

"There's nothing wrong with dreams," Sandra said softly.

"Until they jump up to smack you a good one when they don't come true," David said, turning his head back and closing his eyes. "It's halfway cool out here tonight, isn't it? If it wasn't for the mosquitos I'd sleep right here. Why do I keep saying that? The damnable mosquitos are here to stay."

Are you? Sandra thought, staring at him. She rested one fingertip lightly on her lips, savoring the memory of the sweet, gentle kiss she and David had shared to mark the end of their fussing at each other about the timing of discovering the identity of the benefactor.

Oh, David, she thought, feeling tears prickling at the back of her eyes, I wish I could believe that you are here to stay, guaranteed, just like the mosquitos.

Chapter Ten

Early the next afternoon while the twins were still at church and Sandra was at Saunders, David called his friend Larry Willcox, the Realtor who had the listing for the empty store connected to the Westport's. David taped a sign on the emporium door saying he was next door and if someone wanted to buy anything just rap on the window of the empty building.

"You're a trusting soul," Larry said, after the reading the note. "Come on. Let's take a look at this empty place before you get robbed blind."

"Betcha a buck not one thing gets taken from the store," David said, entering the empty building.

"You're on."

David shoved his hands into the pockets of his slacks and wandered slowly around the large expanse. There was a restroom at the far end, as well as a large storage area where free-standing metal shelves had been left behind.

Larry was knocking on the wall that separated this building from the emporium.

"No problem," he said finally. "You could punch through here with nothing falling down around your ears. Man, this is twice the space you have now. You're talking about a mighty big store, buddy."

"Mmm," David said.

"I can probably get the owner to come down on the price," Larry continued. "He's tired of paying the taxes on this place and it's been empty for a long time now. Have you approached a bank about adding this mortgage to the one you have on your store?"

"No," David said.

"Well, you should if you want to do this. You know, get prequalified, David, so you don't run into a snag once your offer is accepted by the owner."

David nodded.

"So, what do you think?" Larry said.

"Larry, are there any code restrictions on this strip mall?"

"Nope, you can bring whatever you want to in here. A couple of women were looking at this place last year with the idea of opening a pet grooming business, but they decided it was too big, way more space than they needed." Larry laughed. "Anything goes, as long as it doesn't bring the cops knocking on your door."

"Do you have a clue as to how much the owner will lower the price?" David said.

"I can feel him out for you, see what he's got to say," Larry said, shrugging. "He's ready to unload it big time so I'd guess he's open to serious discussion about the price. He and his wife are retired, living in Florida and want out from under the taxes and insurance they're carrying here. Plus, they have utility bills every month because I can't show it well without lights and what have you. Yeah, they'll be open-minded about a low-ball offer."

"Well, I haven't had time to really sit down with Sandra and talk this through. I'll get back to you as soon as I can, though."

"Fair enough. I…"

A knock on the window caused both men to turn. A woman was peering in, then pointed to the plastic basket she was holding that was filled with items from the emporium.

David smiled at Larry, then headed toward the door.

"You owe me a buck, Willcox," David said.

"Yeah, I do," Larry said. "I'm impressed. There are a lot of low income families in the North End, you know, and a basket full of food for free has to be tempting."

"True," David said, opening the door, "but you're forgetting that there are very fine people living in the North End, my friend. Thanks for opening up this place for me."

"Sure. Keep me posted."

Sandra arrived home from Saunders early enough to pick up the twins from church and make dinner, which was ready to put on the table when David walked through the door.

"Hi," he said, dropping a quick kiss on her lips. "Make any major discoveries today?"

"No, darn it," Sandra said, sighing. "How was your day at the store?"

"Fine. I'll wash up. Where are the kids?"

"Playing Ping-Pong. David, I told Rachel I would only be able to come in to help her three days a week, and I had to leave early enough to beat the rush-hour traffic. I'll only go again on Thursday this week, then Monday, Wednesday and Friday next week."

"Okay. Yeah. Good," David said, nodding. "I'll go wash up. Where are the kids?"

Sandra frowned. "I just told you. They're in the kitchen playing Ping-Pong."

"Makes sense. They're training for the Olympics, you know."

Sandra cocked her head to one side and watched David until he disappeared from view.

He's very preoccupied, she thought. What was David focusing on in that complicated mind of his? She had a sinking feeling that she really didn't want to know.

David's I-look-like-I'm-here-but-I'm-really-not performance continued through the dinner, with Sandra very aware that he didn't have second helpings which was his normal habit.

"Okay, Dad?" Michael said.

"What?" David said. "I'm sorry, Michael. I didn't hear what you said."

"I asked you if you'd play Ping-Pong with me after dinner?" Michael said.

"Oh. Hey, not tonight, buddy. I have to go out for a while."

"You do?" Sandra said, looking at him in surprise.

"Yeah, I need to go back to the store for a bit," David said, not looking at her.

"Why?"

"Because I do, Sandra," he said, a slight edge to his voice.

"That's fine," she said. "I was just asking, not grilling you, David."

"How about you, Mom?" Michael said. "Want to try some Ping-Pong?"

"Well, sure, I'll give it a whirl."

"I'll play the winner," Molly said.

"You've been playing against me ever since we got home from church," Michael said.

"Hey, who says you're the guaranteed winner," Sandra said. "I've played this game before, I'll have you know. Yes, I certainly have."

"When?" Michael said.

Sandra laughed. "When I went to Girl Scout camp when I was twelve."

"Lame," Michael said, rolling his eyes. "When was the last time you played Ping-Pong, Dad?"

David didn't reply.

"Dad?"

"Huh?"

"Jeez, Dad," Michael said, frowning, "aren't you listening to anything we're saying here?"

"That's what happens to old people, Michael," Molly said. "They have brain blips, just zone out because what is being said hits a part of their brain that's not working anymore. My friend Ginger says her grandpa has brain blips all the time."

"I'm not having brain blips," David said, chuckling. "I just…just have a lot on my mind right now. I apologize for not paying attention. What did I miss?"

"A whole bunch of stuff about Ping-Pong," Sandra said. "Who wants dessert?"

"I'll pass," David said, getting to his feet. "I'm going to take off. You kids help your mom with the cleanup here before you bring the board back out to play the pong and the ping. See you later."

"But…" Sandra said, but David was already striding from the room. "I made your favorite dessert," she mumbled. "Whoopee."

David drove his clunky old pickup to the far side of town, realizing that if he'd ever been over there it was years before because nothing looked familiar.

Dusk was just beginning to cast shadows over the area as the last of the sunset began to sink below the horizon. David slowed his speed and swept his gaze from one side of the street to the other.

Grim, he thought. Everything looked so…tired, just shabby and worn-out. These were tenements, there was no other word for the connected, four-story apartment buildings that lined the cracked, weed-growing sidewalks for several blocks. Narrow steps led to the entrance of each structure and people were just beginning to emerge to sit on the stoops after their evening meal, such as it might have been.

David drove to the end of the block, turned around and came back slowly, still scrutinizing everything within his view.

Ah, here they come, he thought. The kids. Baggy pants and shirts, baseball caps on backward, they were taking their positions, leaning against the light posts. The Street Corner Crew.

David parked the truck next to the curb and strolled toward four boys, who straightened and narrowed their eyes as he approached. "Hey," David said, when he reached them.

Fourteen or fifteen years old, he thought. Trying so hard to look tough and cool and not quite pulling it off.

"Yeah?" one of the boys said.

"I want to ask you something," David said.

"You a cop?" another boy said.

"No way, man," the third youth said. "Cops don't want no part of bein' seen in a ride that trashy."

"Whoa," David said, smiling. "That truck is my pride and joy."

"Yeah, well," a boy said, "only good thing about it I can see is that you don't got to worry 'bout it getting ripped 'cause nobody would want it."

"What you after, man?" the tallest boy said.

"I was just wondering," David said, "if you guys have anywhere down here to play baseball, basketball...I don't know...sports. Ping-Pong even."

"Why?"

"Because standing around on the corner," David said, "looks boring as hell to me. Aren't you guys into sports at all?"

One of the boys shrugged. "No place to play nothing. Too bad 'cause I can shoot baskets, man. Michael Jordan would eat his heart out watching me scope that hoop."

"Yeah, right, Tony," a boy said, with a shout of laughter. "You're so full of bull. My little brother could outshoot you and he's four years old."

"Hey, you know they got Ping-Pong in the Olympics?" a boy said, twisting one hand this way and that. "Blam, wham, spin that baby. I'd be good at that. I'd like that game 'cause I'm not into sweatin' on no basketball court. Damages my do." He patted his slicked-backed hair.

"Jink, you are talking trash," Tony said. "I could whip your butt playing Ping-Pong. That's after I won twenty games of horse on the b-court."

"Enough of this," the tallest boy said. "Why you askin' 'bout this stuff, dude?"

"Like I said," David said, "I was just wondering what the deal was down here. Doesn't seem quite fair that there's nowhere for you guys to play sports. What about in school? Anything going on there?"

"Nope," Tony said. "There's no money for equipment and junk. Hell, I sit on the floor in two of my classes 'cause we're so smashed in there they ran out of desks. All I learn is how to get a sore butt every day."

"Suppose there was a place for you to play sports on the other side of town," David said. "Would you come?"

"Oh, yeah, man," Tony said. "I'd just drive my BMW right over there and shoot them hoops. Give me a break."

David nodded and stared into space for a long moment.

"Bus passes," he finally said slowly. "You could get over there if you had free bus passes."

"Sure 'nuff," Tony said, with a snort. "I got a pocket full of free bus passes right now. I'm just decidin' where I want to go. Hey, there's nothing free down here, man."

"Ever play baseball?" David said. "I played. I was good, really good."

"Now, there's a game," one of the boys said, pretending he was swinging a bat. "Over the wall. Home run with two out in the ninth and the bases loaded. The whole team is at home plate waitin' for me to come 'round those bases so they can give me the high-five. Cool."

"Picture this," David said, holding his hands up to make an imaginary frame. "A baseball team from down here and you're The Street Corner Crew. That's on the back of your uniforms. The Street Corner Crew. That says you came from here, and that's fine, and you're good, man, you are some kind of baseball players."

"Right on," Tony said, punching one fist in the air. "The Street Corner Crew. And we're hot." He shook his head. "Never goin' to happen, dude. Uniforms? Bats, balls, gloves, all that junk a catcher wears? Sure 'nuff. I got that stuff in the trunk of my BMW. Why are you here talkin' 'bout this? From the looks of your ride, man, you don't got that kind of stuff, neither."

"No, I don't," David said quietly. "But it's payback time, fellas, and I'm thinking about how to get it all."

"Payback time?" Jink said. "Who you owe?"

"I don't know," David said.

"You're not making a whole bunch of sense, man," Tony said. "Don't appreciate your comin' down here blowing smoke about stuff we're not never goin' to have so you just shuffle on off to Buffalo, dude."

"Yeah, okay, I'm going," David said, "but I'll be back. Somehow. You know, Tony, there's nothing wrong with having dreams."

"Down here there is," Tony said, suddenly looking very young and very sad. "Can't even dream 'bout getting out of this hood."

David nodded, then walked slowly back to his truck, deep in thought. As he drove away he looked in the rearview mirror and saw Tony shooting an imaginary ball at an invisible basket and Jinx swinging an imaginary bat.

"I'll be back," David whispered.

Sandra hung up the receiver to the telephone with a shaking hand, then managed to make it to a chair in the living room on legs that threatened to give way beneath her.

Dear heaven, no, she thought, struggling against tears that prickled at the back of her eyes. She'd realized she was low on milk, had called the emporium to ask David to bring some home, only to be told by Benjamin Franklin Capelli that David wasn't there, nor had Ben seen him since he left before dinner time.

David had said he was going to the store, she thought frantically, but that was not where he'd gone. Where was he? What was he doing? Dear God, he'd lied to her. To her, the kids, his family. He'd lied.

He'd been so preoccupied before dinner and all through the meal, then had left the house again as quickly as possible as soon as he'd eaten.

Sandra drew a shuddering breath.

Left the house, she thought, to…to keep a rendezvous with another woman? What other explanation was there for the lie he had told about needing to go back to the store? Oh, David, no. No, no, no.

"Mom!" Michael yelled from the kitchen, causing Sandra to jerk in her chair. "Are you going to come play Ping-Pong, or what?"

"Yes, Michael, I'll be right there," she called. "I'm just finishing… I'm on my way, sweetheart."

Michael beat his mother easily and, as promised, Molly played the winner while Sandra settled onto a chair and watched. She actually managed to blank her mind, not think, not think, not think, because if she did, she knew, she would burst into brokenhearted tears and she had no intention of doing that in front of the twins.

Michael won the game against Molly, then came around the makeshift table and with patience that amazed Sandra and filled her with pride, coached his sister on how to turn the paddle just so and put a spin on the little white ball.

When darkness finally pushed the last of the vibrant sunset below the horizon, Sandra called a halt to the activity.

"Enough for today, cute stuffs," she said. "Let's get the board back under the bed."

"Snack time," Michael said.

"It hasn't been that long since you had two helpings of dessert," Sandra said.

"But I'm hungry for a snack," Michael said, pushing up his end of the board while Molly got the other end.

"You're just like your father," Sandra said, ruffling her son's hair. "You have a bottomless pit. Okay. Snack time it is."

The kids staggered out of the kitchen with their cargo and Sandra stood statue still.

Michael was just like his father? she thought. No, he wasn't. Michael didn't lie. Michael didn't close himself off behind self-constructed walls. Michael didn't wish he lived anywhere else but there with his family. No, Michael wasn't like David, not one little bit.

The twins had their snack, took turns taking their nightly baths, then sprawled in front of the television in their pajamas. Sandra settled onto the sofa, attempting and failing to concentrate on a book she was in the middle of reading.

David entered the apartment about halfway through the show the pair on the floor was watching.

"Hi, gang," he said.

The twins each raised a hand in greeting, their gaze riveted on the television screen.

"Any of that dessert I saw on the counter left?" David asked Sandra.

"No," she said, not looking up from her book. "The kids finished it for their snack."

"Oh. Whatever. I'll have ice cream. Want some?"

"No."

As David went on toward the kitchen, Sandra watched him and was aware of a hot fury pushing aside the chilling pain within her.

How dare he just waltz back in here and decide to have some dessert? she thought. How dare he arrive with a cheerful greeting as though everything was as it should be? Just who in the blue blazes did David Westport think he was?

Sandra snapped the book closed, tossed it on the cushion next to her, got to her feet and marched into the kitchen. David was serving up a cereal bowl full of ice cream.

"Sure you don't want some of this?" he said, glancing at Sandra.

"No, David, I don't want ice cream. What I want is the truth. I called the store to ask you to bring home some milk and Ben said you hadn't been there since you left before dinner. You lied about going to the emporium, didn't you? You knew when you said it that you had no intention of going back to the store. Isn't that right, David?"

David sighed, put the carton of ice cream back in the freezer, picked up the bowl, then set it back onto the counter. He shoved his hands into the pockets of his slacks and stared down at the floor for a long moment before meeting Sandra's furious gaze.

"Yes, that's right," he said quietly. "I didn't tell you the truth about where I knew I was really going."

Sandra wrapped her hands around her elbows as a shiver coursed through her.

"Where did you go?" she said, hardly above a whisper. "Who were you with?"

"I…" He pulled his hands from his pockets and reached toward her. Sandra took a step backward. "I'm not ready to talk about it yet. Ah, please, Sandra, trust me here."

"Trust you? You lied to me. To your children." Tears filled Sandra's eyes. "But you're not ready to give me an explanation for that lie? You're not ready? And I'm supposed to say, oh, sure, David, no problem? You were with a woman, weren't you? You lied about going to the store, then you kept a prearranged meeting with…with a…"

"No," he said, taking a step forward and gripping her shoulders. "God, Sandra, how can even think such a thing? I've never cheated on you. I wouldn't do that. Not ever. I…I just needed some time…alone. I've got so damn much on my mind and I'm trying to work it all through and figure out how to… I was not with a woman. You've got to believe me when I say that."

"Do I?" she said, lifting her chin and ignoring the two tears that slid down her cheeks. "Just automatically believe a man who lied so he could get out the door? No, it doesn't work that way, David."

"Sandra…"

"Are you having a fight?" Molly said, from the kitchen doorway. "Are you mad at each other?"

David dropped his hands from Sandra's shoulders, moved around her and went to where his daughter was staring at them with a stricken expression on her face. Sandra swiped the tears from her cheeks, then turned slowly to look at the pair.

"No, sugarplum," David said to Molly, "we're not fighting. Your ol' Dad was pulling a tantrum because you piggy-wiggies ate all the special dessert and I'm stuck with ice cream. Shame on me. I was acting about three years old about that dessert. It was my favorite, you rotten kid."

Molly giggled. "You should have had some before you went back to the store. You snooze, you lose."

"You're right," David said. "I learned my lesson, big time. What are you and Michael watching on the tube?"

"It's cool. It's about this giant spider that's gobbling up everything and stuff, and the good guys are trying to stop it from eating Chicago and…"

"Sounds great," David said. "Come on. I'll watch it with you two."

"'Kay," Molly said, then they headed toward the living room. "The spider is super gross, Dad. It's got these big eyes and it's hairy and junk…"

Sandra watched them go, then turned to see that the ice cream David had served up was slowly melting into a puddle in the bowl.

The ice cream had looked so appealing, so perfect, she thought, feeling as though she was floating outside of herself, wasn't really there in that kitchen. But now? The ice cream wasn't what it once was. No. Now it was a mess that no one would want any part of. And the really sad thing about the ice cream was that it couldn't be fixed, the damage was done. It was ruined. Would never be the same again.

Chapter Eleven

After a nearly sleepless night with no words exchanged with his wife, David left the bed shortly after dawn and stood looking across the rumpled sheets at Sandra's back.

"I'll get the kids fed and drive them to the church," he said quietly. "You try to get some sleep. I know you were awake as much as I was last night."

He paused and dragged both hands down his beard-roughened face. "Sandra, I did not cheat on you, I swear it. I'm very, very sorry that I lied to you about going back to the store. I should have just said that I needed time to try to sort through everything that's happened and…I'm sorry I did it the way I did."

He shook his head. "I guess I was on a macho trip for a moment and thought it sounded wimpy to say I needed some space, some private time or whatever. Hell, I don't know why I did what I did. Lied. It's like…it's like I suddenly have this giant puzzle to put together and I can't get the pieces to fit and… Ever since I found out about the benefactor I… Please, Sandra, trust me. Please."

David waited, but Sandra didn't move, nor speak.

With a sigh that seemed to come from his very soul, David walked slowly toward the bathroom. Sandra pretended to be asleep until David had left the bedroom, then rolled onto her back and stared up at the ceiling.

The benefactor, her mind echoed. The damnable benefactor. Yes, okay, she knew David was basically unhappy being with her, their lifestyle, what he had had to settle for when his dreams had been wiped off the map by her pregnancy.

But he'd been hanging in there, was devoted to the twins, was such a wonderful father. But, no, he no longer loved her as evidenced by the fact that she couldn't remember the last time he had told her he loved her.

Sandra curled her hands into fists and slammed them onto the sheet that covered her.

But now because of the summons from Professor Harrison to attend the pseudo reunion at Saunders and his revealing of the existence of the benefactor, it was all coming to a head. David was scrutinizing his life, detail by detail, and obviously didn't like what he was being forced to face.

Oh, he was trying, she knew that now. Had said he was attempting to put things back together like a giant puzzle. But the pieces didn't fit. It wasn't working, and even though he'd asked her to trust him, he'd reach the conclusion that he...

"Oh, God," Sandra whispered, pressing her fingertips to her throbbing temples. "He's going to leave. I know he is. I just know it."

Sandra flopped back over onto her stomach and despite her upset, finally dozed, the long hours of the night that she'd spent staring into the darkness catching up with her. When she woke several hours later the house was silent, so very, very quiet.

She showered and dressed in jeans and a cotton sport top, then called her friend Cindy Morrison, who had been away on vacation since shortly after the bake sale at church where they'd last talked. They made a date to meet for lunch at one of their favorite casual restaurants, Cindy saying she could get her teenage neighbor to baby-sit for a couple of hours.

Unable to sit still until it was time to leave for the

lunch date, Sandra dashed off an article for the paper on the subject of when women wouldn't dream of being seen in public for a social engagement without wearing a hat and short white gloves. It had been a more serene era, more feminine and refined that had disappeared when women decided they wanted to take their place in the male world.

"Who gives a royal rip?" she said, rolling her eyes as she pressed the send button on the e-mail program. "Whatever."

She did a load of wash, prepared a casserole she could pop in the oven for dinner, then finally, finally it was time to meet Cindy.

At the restaurant the two women exchanged hugs, ordered chicken salad, cheese biscuits and iced tea, Cindy gave a brief report on the vacation trip, then narrowed her eyes and stared at Sandra.

"You look like hell," Cindy said, after their lunches were set in front of them. "What's wrong? What's going on, Sandra?"

And Sandra told her.

She poured out her heart to her best friend, blinking back tears at times as she related everything that had happened.

"David is getting ready to leave me, Cindy," she said finally. "This business with the benefactor has made it impossible for him to push all his disappointment and sense of failure into the background any longer. He's so unhappy, so dissatisfied with me, our life together and…" She shook her head.

"That benefactor guy is a creep," Cindy said. "To give people gifts, then wait ten years and… That is rotten, really nasty. Let's find him and shoot him."

Sandra produced a wobbly little laugh. "Good idea. No, it isn't, because it's too late. The damage is done."

"I still find it hard to believe that David doesn't love you. No, I can't buy that. Yes, he's struggling emotionally right now but… Look, here's my advice for what it's worth. Be patient. Give him time to deal with all of this. He's… how did he put it?…trying to put the pieces of the puzzle together.

"Okay. Let him do that in his dumb-as-a-post male way. He lied to you last night, the dolt, because he was afraid it wouldn't sound macho to say he needed private time and space. Men are so icky about emotional upheavals. Blak. Anyway, you just keep on keeping on, and let him work it all through."

"We should be doing it together," Sandra said, leaning forward. "He's shutting me out completely, building those walls around himself so high, so strong and… Oh, Cindy, what if he comes to the conclusion that he just can't live with me anymore, can't—"

"Eat your lunch," Cindy interrupted. "I don't want to hear you say again that David Westport doesn't love you because he does. I know he does."

"No, he…"

"Stuff some chicken in your mouth, Sandra. You're going to be Ms. Sunshine in that house. Ignore his dark mood and do things as you normally would, smiling your little heart out. Do that for you, for the kids and for David. It will all work out just fine, you'll see." Cindy smiled. "And if David actually ends up doing something really stupid, we'll shoot him, too."

"Oh, okay," Sandra said, with a genuine burst of laughter. "Thank you, Cindy. You're such a good friend. I don't know what I'd do without you."

"I feel the same way about you," Cindy said, nodding. "That's where men make just one of their mistakes. They bottle things up inside instead of talking it all through like women do. That's just the way the dumb-dumbs are. Remember now, be patient and smile. Got that?"

"Be patient and smile." Sandra sighed. "But what if David…"

"Sandra!"

"Okay, okay, be patient and smile."

"Good girl. For that you get to have a sinfully fattening dessert, and because I'm such a super friend I'll sin right along with you."

Sandra had sent the twins to wash their hands and was putting dinner on the table when David arrived home that evening.

"Hello, hello," she sang out as he entered the kitchen. "How was your day? I saw Cindy. They had a wonderful time on their vacation. She's tan and gorgeous, of course. Wash up, okay? This casserole is piping hot and ready to be devoured. I made a nice fruit salad to go with it, too. Are you hungry? Dumb question. You're always hungry. So. Here we go. Dinner is served and…"

"Sandra," David said quietly.

"Hmm?" she said, raising her eyebrows as she looked at him.

"Is this motormouth thing your way of saying you forgive me for what I did last night?"

"Oh, sure," she said breezily. "It was a rotten thing to do, you understand, but your explanation made sense in a dopey male sort of way. It's over. Done. Kaput."

"Thank you," he said, then washed his hands at the kitchen sink. "I mean that. I'm really sorry."

"Apology accepted."

"Hi, Dad," Michael said, coming into the kitchen and sliding onto his chair.

"Hey, Ping," David said, drying his hands on a paper towel. "Where's Pong?"

Molly appeared, sat down and peered at the casserole.

"Oh, not that thing," she said. "I hate it. Do I have to eat that stuff?"

"Nope," Sandra said, setting the fruit salad on the table. "You can starve if you prefer. It's up to you. That happens to be one of your father's favorite casseroles."

"I suppose it's better than nothing," Molly said, with a dramatic sigh.

"Cork it, Pong," David said, taking his place at the table. "You're lucky to have a mother who puts a delicious meal on the table every night. Some kids just have to wing it."

"That would be cool," Molly said, putting a minuscule serving of the casserole on her plate. "Everybody just fix what they want."

"You'd die of scurvy," David said, ladling up a huge portion of the offering.

"I like this junk," Michael said, reaching for the dish.

"Thanks. I think," Sandra said.

They ate in silence for several minutes, no one commenting when Molly put more of the casserole on her plate.

"I have news," David said finally. "I got on the phone today and here's the scoop. Mr. Morales is going to be coaching the girl's soccer team this year and Mr. Gambini will take over the little league baseball."

Sandra dropped her fork. "What?"

"Why?" the twins said in unison.

"I've coached both teams for several years now," David said, adding some more fruit salad to his plate.

"It's time to pass the baton, as I've recently learned. Other dads can do the job just as well, if not better, than I can and they were willing to take it on. You two can decide later if you want to play or if you're going to concentrate on the Ping-Pong thing. Whatever you decide is fine."

"Oh," Michael said, shrugging. "'Kay."

"Mr. Morales is nice," Molly said, nodding. "Tina Morales is one of my friends, you know, from the soccer team. Her dad tells knock-knock jokes all the time."

David chuckled. "Can't ask for more than that. If you want to play soccer again this year, Molly, that's fine. If not, that's okay, too."

"I'll think about it," she said. "I'm really into Ping-Pong now, but I'm waiting to see if it'll get boring."

"That's lame," Michael said. "There's no way that Ping-Pong can get boring, Molly Mud-brain."

"Well, we'll just see about that, Michael Microbe," Molly said, glaring at her brother. "Maybe it will and maybe it won't."

"Oh, yeah?" Michael shot back.

Sandra tuned out the bickering between the twins and forced herself to take another bite of her dinner that now tasted like sawdust.

David was clearing his decks, she thought frantically. He was seeing that all his obligations were tended to before he left and… Oh, dear God, no.

"Chill," she heard David say, and forced her attention back to what was taking place at the table.

"But, Dad," Michael said.

"No more," David said. "You're arguing with each other out of habit, nothing more. Knock it off or you can forget about dessert." He laughed. "Molly Mud-brain? Michael Microbe? Actually that's pretty good stuff, but I don't want to hear it again."

"Okay," the twins said together, then laughed along with their father.

David was such a wonderful daddy, Sandra thought, giving up the effort to eat. The twins deserved so much more than a weekend father, snatches of time with David. But that's what would happen when David packed up and left.

"Hey, Sandra," David said, glancing over at her. "Aren't you feeling well? You hardly touched your dinner."

"Oh, I'm fine," she said, producing a small smile. "I had a big lunch with Cindy today, that's all. We so rarely go out to eat together and we made the most of it."

David nodded, and the remainder of the meal was spent in back and forth conversation which included everyone but Sandra. The twins cleared the table after consuming chocolate frosted brownies along with David, then he joined them outside on the stoop while Sandra put the finishing touches on cleaning the kitchen.

She wandered into the living room and turned on the television to watch the evening news, not hearing one word the anchorwoman said. Hearing only David's announcement that he had found replacements for his coaching positions of the kids' sport teams.

One would think, she thought finally, folding her arms beneath her breasts, that David would have told her about a major decision like that before just tossing it out on the dinner table in front of the entire family. Coaching took up a lot of hours that he was now freeing up and…

Oh, who was she kidding? Why should he talk it over with her? She was so low on his list of importance. He had been informing the twins of his decision because he had been their coach. As far as David was concerned, it had nothing to do with her.

As darkness fell, the trio came back into the house, and Sandra turned the television remote over to the twins. David sat on the opposite end of the sofa from her and read the newspaper, humming off-key.

Well, aren't we just a happy fella? Sandra fumed. And why not? He'd just taken care of one of the things on the list he no doubt had made regarding what needed doing before he could leave and the kids hadn't been the least bit upset about his announcement.

Time dragged slowly by. Sandra waited and

waited for David to comment on something he was reading as he usually did, but he didn't speak, nor look at her.

Sandra finally announced it was time to start baths and Molly jumped up and said she was first.

"No way," Michael yelled. "How come you always…"

David cleared his throat and the twins looked at him quickly.

"Yeah, okay," Michael said, directing his attention to the television screen again. "I'm not losing my snack because of her."

"Good thinking, buddy," David said. "You have to keep your priorities straight, know what's important."

"Like you do?" Sandra said, hearing the edge to her voice.

"What?" David said, looking over at her.

"Nothing," she said, sighing. "I'm going to go make some notes for my next article for the newspaper. I have to come up with something better than the one I just turned in, that's for sure."

As Sandra got to her feet the telephone rang.

"I'll get it in the kitchen," she said, quickening her step.

Once there she snatched up the receiver. "Hello?"

"Oh… Hello, Sandra," a man said. "This is Gilbert Harrison. May I speak to David, please?"

No, she thought sullenly. Haven't you done

enough damage delivering the dictates from the crummy, unknown benefactor?

"Yes, certainly," she said. "Just a moment, please."

She called David to the telephone, told him who was calling, then returned to her spot on the sofa, deciding she didn't have one intelligent thought regarding an article for the *North End News*.

"Professor Harrison?" David said, after taking the receiver.

"Yes," Gilbert said. "I'm sorry to disturb your evening with your family, David, but it's imperative that I speak with you."

"No problem. Go ahead."

"No, I'd rather meet with you in person."

David sighed and dragged a restless hand through his hair.

"Professor Harrison," he said, "if the benefactor is demanding an update already on what I've done toward paying back my gift you can tell him I have nothing to report. Passing the baton is not all that easy."

"No, no, this has nothing to do with the benefactor," Gilbert said.

"Then what…"

"David, could you possibly meet me for dinner tomorrow evening? I'd be more than willing to drive to the North End so you don't have to come all the way in here."

"Well, sure, I guess so," David said, frowning.

"Good, that's good. Tell me where I should meet you. Say, seven o'clock?"

David picked a quiet Italian restaurant and gave the professor directions to where it was located.

"Fine. I'll see you there," Gilbert said. "Goodbye, David."

"Goodbye," David said, then hung up the receiver.

Sandra came into the kitchen to find David staring at the telephone.

"David?" she said. "What's wrong?"

"Huh?" he said, spinning around. "Oh, nothing. Or something. I don't know. Professor Harrison wants to talk to me but says it has nothing to do with the benefactor. He's going to drive out here tomorrow night and we're meeting for dinner at seven. I have no clue as to what is on his mind."

"That's weird," Sandra said, frowning. "Well, I'm going into Saunders tomorrow to work with Rachel again, but I'll be home before the rush hour so... What do you suppose Professor Harrison wants now?"

"Like I said, I haven't a clue."

"Well, I'm not going to give him the satisfaction of asking him if I see him in his office tomorrow," Sandra said, walking to the refrigerator and yanking open the freezer. She removed the ice-cream carton. "Dear heaven, I'm sick to death of men and their secrets."

"What's that supposed to mean?" David said,

following her to the counter where she was setting out bowls.

"Well, for one thing," she said, turning to face him, "I don't think I should have heard your announcement about your choosing to quit coaching the kids' teams at the same time the twins did. That is a major decision, David, and I would think you would have discussed it with me."

"And say what?" he said, obviously confused. "Exactly what I said at the table, that's what. I made the decision, got replacements for the teams, end of story. There really wasn't anything to discuss."

"Oh, never mind," she said, scooping out some ice cream and plopping it into one of the bowls.

"This is a woman thing, right?" he said. "I should have told you first even though you don't play on either the soccer or the softball team. You didn't like hearing it at the same time as the kids because... Yep, it's a woman thing, which means I won't live long enough to understand it."

Sandra decided to count to ten before she said another word. She got all the way to five, then gave up the battle against her frustration and bubbling anger. She filled the spoon with ice cream, reached over and pulled the neck of David's T-shirt forward and dumped in the cold dessert. In the next instant she gave the sliding ice cream a firm smack with the flat of her hand.

David's mouth dropped open in shock and his arms shot out stiffly to the sides, giving him the appearance of an astonished scarecrow.

"That's what I think of your *woman's thing* malarkey, Mr. Westport," Sandra said, poking her nose in the air.

"I... Oh... Cold..." David sputtered, as a large wet pattern spread on his shirt. "I can't believe you did that. Are you nuts? Oh, man, that is so cold."

David pulled the shirt away from his chest with the tips of two fingers, groaning as the ice cream slid lower.

And Sandra laughed. She laughed until she had to wrap her arms around her stomach and take a gulp of air as she watched David's performance. Every time she thought she was under control she looked at him again and burst into renewed laughter.

David attempted to remove the shirt by pulling his arms inward so he wouldn't have to draw the sticky mess up and over his head, but the effort failed, and Sandra fell apart with a loud hoot of merriment.

The noise finally brought the pajama-clad twins into the kitchen to investigate what was going on.

"Wow, Dad," Michael said, staring at David's shirt. "What happened to you?"

"Your father," Sandra said, then hiccuped, "had a slight accident with a scoop of ice cream."

"I don't see any ice cream," Molly said, peering

at her dad's shirt. Just wet something." She pressed a fingertip against the T-shirt. "Cold something."

"The ice cream," Sandra said, flapping one hand in the air, "sort of landed inside the shirt."

"I get it, I get it, I get it," Molly said, jumping up and down like a pogo-stick. "Mom put ice cream inside Dad's shirt." She stopped jumping and frowned. "How come?"

"Oh, that is so-o-o not cool," Michael said, awe ringing in his voice. "Wow."

"Wrong," David said, a smile beginning to tug at the corners of his lips. "It's beyond cool, Michael. It's well on its way to frostbite." He laughed and shook his head. "Well, one thing can be said for the Westport household. It's never dull around here."

"I don't understand grown-ups sometimes," Michael said to Molly.

"Me, neither," she said.

"I have a question, family," Sandra said.

All eyes shifted to Sandra.

She waved the spoon in the air.

"One scoop," she said, smiling, "or two?"

The next day when Sandra arrived at Saunders she found a note from Rachel on the desk in the office. She'd been up most of the night with a toothache, Rachel wrote, and after coming into the office for a while, gave up and found a dentist who would fit her in and solve the problem. She'd see Sandra the following Monday.

Sandra peered across the hall and saw that Professor Harrison's door was closed. She narrowed her eyes and sent him mental messages to emerge and tell her why he had set up the dinner date with David for that evening. The door didn't open. A few minutes later a student came to Gilbert's office, knocked, waited, then walked away.

Professor Harrison wasn't even in there, Sandra thought. The coward. He was probably hiding out at home so she couldn't confront him about the plans for the evening with David. She shook her head, removed a stack of files from the cabinet and settled onto the chair behind the desk.

At noon she strolled to the cafeteria for a hot dog and soda, then returned to examine more files for a clue, something, anything, that would point toward the identity of the benefactor.

When it was time to leave before the rush hour traffic, she had once again accomplished absolutely nothing. She wrote a note to Rachel announcing that dismal news, said she hoped Rachel's dental problem had been solved, glared at the still closed door to Professor Harrison's office, then left the building for the drive home.

Arriving at the North End after battling zany drivers, Sandra picked up the twins at church and listened to their report of their fun day. In the kitchen at home she found a note from David on the table.

"My day for written communications," Sandra muttered, as the kids went to retrieve the board so they could play Ping-Pong.

David was going to work straight through at the store, the note said, since he wouldn't be eating at home. He'd time it so he had the opportunity to shower and change clothes, then meet Professor Harrison at the restaurant.

"What…ever," Sandra said, flipping the note back onto the table.

She opened the refrigerator, frowned at the contents and shut the door. She then repeated the scrutiny with the freezer, unable to smother a bubble of laughter when she spied the ice cream carton. Next stop was her purse where she counted the money in her wallet, nodding in approval.

Forty-five minutes later, to the amazed delight of the twins, a pizza was delivered to the Westport house.

Shortly after six o'clock, David dashed in the front door, yelled that he was running late and headed for the bedroom. Sandra met him in the living room when he reappeared in gray slacks and a pale green dress shirt open at the neck, his hair still damp from his shower.

"Gotta go," he said.

"David, wait a minute," she said. "Please."

"Sure. What is it?"

"I know that Professor Harrison wants to meet privately with you tonight, but… Well, I feel that… What I mean is, I think I have the right…"

"Sandra," David said, framing her face with his hands, "I hereby solemnly swear to tell you exactly what transpires at this dinner meeting with the professor, including what was consumed for the meal, how long it took to get served and every word, including the usual starting off blather about the weather, exchanged between Gilbert Harrison and myself. Okay?"

"Really?" Sandra said brightly.

"Oh, yes, ma'am," he said, grinning at her. "Why? Because my wild, full-of-surprises wife, I have no intention of trying to survive a repeat performance of the ice-cream debacle of last night."

"Oh, that," she said, laughing. "I don't know what came over me."

"Well, I know what came over me and it was very cold stuff. You never did say you were sorry."

"I can't, because I'm not," she said, smiling.

"Fair enough," he said, chuckling. "I'm now going to be late. Bye." He dropped a quick kiss on her lips.

"David?"

"Yeah?"

"I know you're being silly about being afraid I'll repeat any ice-cream caper, but kidding aside, don't you think I have the right to know what Professor Harrison discusses with you?"

David looked at his watch and strode toward the door.

"Sure thing," he said absently. "Of course. Yes. See ya."

Sandra sighed as she heard the door close behind David, then sank onto the sofa.

Oh, she'd hear a full report on the reason for the private dinner, she thought glumly, because David didn't want to set her off on a rip again. But he just didn't get it. He didn't seem to grasp the concept of there not being secrets kept between them.

Well, Professor Harrison was no prize package in that department, either, now that she thought about it. By asking to meet with David privately, what was Gilbert actually saying? *This is between us men, son, so leave Sandra at home while we talk.* The man was a generation older and he didn't get it any more than David did.

"Well, why should either of them come out of the ether?" she said, getting to her feet with the intention of playing Ping-Pong with the twins. "After all, silly Sandra, it's a woman thing." She stomped across the room. "Oh-h-h, blak."

Chapter Twelve

Gilbert Harrison was waiting outside the restaurant when David arrived and apologized for being late.

"Not a problem," Gilbert said. "I enjoy people-watching."

"I hope you don't mind having Italian food again," David said, pulling open the door to the restaurant, "but you can't beat what is prepared here in the North End."

Gilbert laughed. "I could eat Italian food seven days a week, to tell you the truth."

"Great," David said, smiling.

They were shown to a booth in the corner, given menus and a few minutes later placed their order.

David folded his arms on the top of the table and looked at Gilbert.

"Could we cut to the chase, sir?" David said. "Why did you ask to meet with me tonight?"

Gilbert sighed. "Well, I'm obviously not going to be able to postpone this with chitchat for a bit."

"No, sir."

"David, please know that I realize that I'm aware that I'm overstepping by what I'm about to relate to you. If at any time you want to tell me to mind my own business, go right ahead. However, my conscience says I have to attempt to do this because…"

"I get the drift," David interrupted, frowning.

"Yes." Gilbert took a deep breath and let it out slowly. "Here we go." He paused. "One day when Sandra and Rachel were going through the files in the office across from mine, I came out of the small room next to it where I make copies. I overhead Sandra and Rachel talking."

David nodded, his gaze riveted on the professor.

"I could have gone on in to my own office," Gilbert continued, "but I stood there and listened to what was being said without them being aware of my presence. I was very upset by what I heard. I've struggled with this, David, and finally decided I had to tell you, then let the chips fall where they may."

"I hope you know you're scaring the hell out of me," David said.

At that moment the waitress appeared with their dinners. The men each took one bite, then set their forks on the sides of their plates.

"Son," Gilbert said, his voice not quite steady, "Sandra was crying that day because she honestly believes, well, she believes that you...that you no longer love her. That perhaps you never did."

"What!" David said, much too loudly. Then looked quickly around and lowered his voice before he spoke again. "What in the hell are you saying?"

"I heard her, David. She was devastated, crying as though her heart was breaking. She feels you still blame her for getting pregnant and making it impossible for you to achieve your dream of playing professional baseball and having all that that world would have brought to your existence."

David shook his head as he felt the color drain from his face.

"Sandra told Rachel," Gilbert said, "that the business with the benefactor was the last straw for you, that you were ridden with guilt for wasting your gift and it was her fault. She thinks... Oh, David, not only does she believe you don't love her, but she's convinced you're going to leave her. She said that she can't remember the last time you told her that you love her. She can't remember hearing you speak those words to her."

David's heart beat with such a wild tempo that it

actually hurt and he splayed one hand firmly over it for a moment.

"Sandra," he said, then cleared his throat. "Sandra said all this to Rachel?"

Gilbert nodded.

"My God, I can't believe this," David said incredulously. "She thinks I don't love her? She's my life, my other half, my…I can't imagine facing a future without her or… She's convinced I'm going to leave her? *Leave her?* She feels I blame her for getting pregnant all those years ago and…I'm the father of those twins. She didn't get pregnant alone and I wouldn't erase the existence of Michael and Molly for anything in this world. Not love Sandra? That's crazy, absolutely nuts."

"When was the last time you told her that you love her, David?" Professor Harrison said quietly.

"Well, I'm not certain, but I'm sure I said it plenty of times. Yeah, I tell her all the time that I…" David took a shuddering breath. "Don't I? Of course I do. Don't I? God, I don't know." He dragged a trembling hand across his face. "Oh, man, what have I done? My wife believes I don't love her, that I'm getting ready to leave her and I wasn't even aware of how unhappy she was. What kind of a man am I?"

"A typical one, I'd say," Gilbert said with a wry smile. "We men have a tendency to take our wonderful women for granted at times, assume they know how we feel about them because, after all, we're there with them, aren't we?

"But, David, women need more than that. They want, they need, to hear those declarations of love, those heartfelt words we just never quite get around to saying, nor do we think they're really necessary after being together for years.

"My Mary, God bless her, explained all this to me in no uncertain terms and none too quietly very early on in our marriage. She said I didn't have to understand how she felt, but she expected me to respect how she felt. From that moment forward until I lost her, we declared our love for each other every day. Not by rote, not just parroting, but meaning it, and it was good, son. Trust me on this…it was good."

"I've taken Sandra for granted," David said, staring into space. "Everything she does for me, the kids—I just expect her to keep on doing it. Do you know that I like to watch her sleep? She's so beautiful, my Sandra, so very lovely and I love her so much, so damn much. But I can't…I can't remember the last time I told her that."

"Is there something wrong with your dinners, gentlemen?" the waitress said, appearing suddenly at the table.

"What?" David said, snapping his head around to look at her. "Dinners? Oh, dinners. No, they're fine. Great. We're just not as hungry as we thought we were."

"Well, I can warm them up if you'd like," the young woman said.

"No, thanks," Gilbert said. "We're fine."

"Wait a minute," David said. "You're wearing a wedding band."

The waitress held out her left hand and looked at the ring. "Yes?"

"When was the last time your husband told you that he loved you?" David said.

"I beg your pardon?" she said, frowning.

"Humor me, please. This is extremely important," David said.

"Well, he told me before I left the house to come on duty here. He does that every night before I leave. I'm waiting tables so he can finish college and he appreciates the fact that it's hard work. He thanks me at the most unexpected moments, says how much he loves me, and we talk about how it will all be worth it in the future when he gets his degree. Does that answer your question?"

"Yeah," David said miserably. "Hang onto that guy. He's a rare man among men, I think."

"I know," she said, laughing. "He's mine and I'm keeping him. Well, let me know if there's anything you need to go with this meal you no longer want."

The waitress walked away and David pushed his plate to one side, knowing he wouldn't be able to choke down another bite.

"It would seem," Gilbert said, "that all I've done lately is upset you and I'm extremely sorry about that. First there was my news about the benefactor and now this. I hope you're not angry that I've stepped right into the middle of your marriage."

"No, no, sir, I'm very grateful to you for going to all the trouble to meet with me, tell me what you heard Sandra telling Rachel. Man, I am batting zero all the way around the block in every arena of my life." David produced a small, fleeting smile. "Well, my kids still think I'm cool, for an old man with brain blips, that is." He dragged both hands down his face. "Ah, what a mess. I've blown it. Big time."

"Then set things to rights, David."

"How do I do that?" he said, turning his hands palm up. "Say something like, 'Oh, by the way, Sandra, I keep forgetting to tell you that I love you. So, I love you. There you go, patootie. Now everything is great'? What if…dear God, what if I've destroyed Sandra's love for me because I've been such a jerk?"

"David, slow down and think," Gilbert said, leaning forward. "Would she be so devastated if she no longer cared, if she no longer loved you, if it no longer mattered to her? No. Talk to her from your heart, tell her how you really feel."

"Why should she trust me, believe me?"

"Because women are wonderful creatures that we men rarely deserve."

"Yeah. Man, I feel like the scum of the earth," David said, shaking his head. "Look, can you get a message to the benefactor?"

"Well, yes," Gilbert said, obviously surprised by the change of topic.

"Tell him that I've been giving this business about payback a great deal of thought, I really have, and I intend to do it…somehow. But make it clear that right now my wife, my marriage comes first, needs my entire attention. That's the message."

"He'll understand," Gilbert said, nodding. "I'll explain things and… Don't worry."

"Thank you." David looked at his watch. "I don't want to go home until I know the twins are asleep, but I need some time to think about what you told me about Sandra. Have the waitress warm your dinner and enjoy your meal, but I've got to leave."

"Go right ahead, David."

David slid out of the booth and stood next to the table.

"Thank you for what you did tonight, sir," he said, extending his hand to Gilbert. "A lot of people wouldn't have taken the time and trouble to do it, would have just shrugged and gone about their own business. I appreciate it more than I can ever begin to put into words."

Gilbert took David's hand in both of his.

"You've always been important to me, David."
He released David's hand. "My thoughts and best
wishes will be with you."

David nodded, then strode away. Gilbert watched
him until he disappeared from view.

"Well, Mary," he said quietly, "I've done all I can
do. Now it's up to David and Sandra."

David drove to a small park that was tucked in the
middle of a neighborhood and deserted at this hour
of the evening. He sank onto a wooden bench, rested
his elbows on his knees and steepled his fingers, resting them against his lips.

He went over and over everything that Professor
Harrison had told him, shaking his head often as he
replayed the words in his mind. Time lost meaning.
Total darkness fell and a million stars sparkled in
the night sky. Mosquitos buzzed and birds sang
their good-night songs, but David was oblivious to
it all.

He finally straightened, flattened his hands on his
thighs and pushed himself to his feet. He strode toward
his car, then stopped as a shiver coursed through him.

He was scared to death, he realized. What if he
poured out his heart to Sandra, begged her to forgive
him for being so...so incredibly stupid only to have
her say it was too little, too late? What if the pain he
had caused her was bigger and stronger than anything

he could say to her to repair the damage he had done? What if he lost his beloved Sandra?

"No," he said, starting off again, nearly running. "No. Please no."

When David entered the apartment he found Sandra in her favorite chenille robe, curled up in the corner of the sofa with a book, her feet tucked up beside her.

"Well, Professor Harrison must have had a great deal to talk to you about," she said, smiling up at David. "You were gone for hours."

David nodded, shoved his hands in to his pockets, pulled them free again, folded his arms, then dropped them to his sides.

"David?" Sandra said, cocking her head slightly to one side. "What's wrong? You're so tense and you're pale, too. Oh, darn that Professor Harrison. What did he say to upset you this time?"

She closed the book, set it on the coffee table and swung her feet around to the floor.

"David?"

"He… God, Sandra, he told me that he heard… He admittedly listened to what was a private conversation and I'm so grateful that he did. I just hope I'm not too late to… Oh, man, where do I start?"

"By making sense?" Sandra said, raising her eyebrows.

"Yeah. Right. I'm just babbling, aren't I?"

Sandra padded the cushion next to her.

"Why don't you sit down and start at the top?" she said.

David sank onto the sofa with a sigh and Sandra shifted so she could look directly at him.

"Okay," she said. "Let's see. Professor Harrison told you that he heard…what?"

"He heard you and Rachel talking in that office where she's working at Saunders. He heard… you…crying, Sandra. He stood outside in the hall and listened to everything that was said."

"What!" she said, nearly shrieking. "How dare he do such a thing? Who does he think he is?"

"A man who cares." David took Sandra's hands in his and looked directly into her eyes. "Listen to me. Okay? I pray I do this right. Hear me out. Please?"

Sandra nodded.

"Honey, I've been such a jerk," David said, his voice gritty with emotion, "and I would have kept right on being a jerk if Professor Harrison hadn't met with me tonight. There's no excuse for my behavior. None.

"Gilbert told me… He said that you think I don't love you anymore, that you believe I blame you because I couldn't play pro ball. He said that you're even convinced that I'm going to leave you."

"He had no right…." Sandra attempted to pull her hands free, but David tightened his grip.

"He said," David continued, "that you couldn't even remember the last time I told you that I love you."

Sandra started to speak, but tears filled her eyes and she shook her head.

"I jumped right in there," David said, "and told Professor Harrison that, of course, I told you that I love you, had said it…but then I realized I couldn't remember when I'd said it. I knew it in my heart, felt it when I looked at you, was filled with it when I watched you sleep, but I hadn't taken the time to stop and tell you.

"And so I'm saying it now, hoping and praying I'm not too late. Sandra Westport, I love you with all that I am as a man. You are my wife, my life, my soul mate, my other half. I love you. I. Love. You."

"Oh, David," she said, then burst into tears. "I thought…I was so sure that you… You could have played baseball and been rich and famous and… The benefactor brought it all to the front of your mind again and… Oh-h-h, I've been so miserable."

David dropped her hands and whipped a handkerchief from his back pocket. Sandra took it and dabbed at her nose.

"Forgive me, please?" David said. "For being so caught up in day-to-day stuff that I didn't tell you each and every day how I feel about you. For taking you for granted. You keep this family on course, running like a smooth machine and I haven't told you how much I appreciate that.

"You never complain about how we never quite have enough money, can't go on fancy vacations, don't have top-of-the-line clothes or... You don't complain about anything and you'd have a right to have a list of grievances a mile long.

"Ah, sweetheart, I can't imagine life without you and our kids. I wish we had the money to have a couple more babies because the father thing is just so great and being your husband has made me the proudest man on this earth."

"Oh, David, I love you so much," Sandra said, tears streaming down her face. "To know that you *do* love me, that you are *not* going to leave me... I'd like more babies, too, but..." She produced a wobbly smile. "I guess we'll just have to wait until we're grandparents to have little ones to bounce on our knees again. Oh, God, David, we're going to get old together, be wrinkled and weird and wonderful."

"You betcha."

"You don't resent not being able to play professional baseball?"

"No, Sandra, no. My dad wanted it for me more than I did. Sure, it would be nice to have the kind of money those guys make, but I'd be on the road so much and, hey, how could I watch you sleep in the moonlight if I was in some hotel across the country? I like having Westport's Emporium. Ah, Sandra, the bottom line is I love you with all my heart and I'm a very, very happy man."

"I love you with all my heart, too, but...David, you've been upset, unhappy, it seems, ever since Professor Harrison told you about the benefactor, about passing the baton to pay back what you received."

David nodded. "I know. I've got to do that, pass the baton, to put the last piece in the puzzle. I've been giving it a great deal of thought and...I messed up there, too, because I convinced myself that I should have it all worked out before I talked it over with you because...because I didn't want to fall short in your eyes, be diminished if my ideas were really too far off the wall. That macho junk got in the way again. I'm sorry."

"You have a plan of sorts?"

"Yeah, but we're not getting into all that tonight. No, not tonight." He framed her face in his hands and gently stoked away her tears. "I want to ask you something."

"Oh...okay."

"Sandra..." David stared up at the ceiling for a moment, then gave up the battle against the tears that filled his own eyes. "Sandra Westport," he continued, his voice ringing with emotion, "will you...will you marry me?"

"Will I… Pardon me?"

"I want us to renew our wedding vows. I want you, the kids, our friends…hell, the whole world…to know how much I love you, how much we love each other. Will you? Marry me? Again? For better, for worse, in sickness and in health, for richer and heaven knows for poorer, until death do us part?"

"Oh, David, yes," she said, smiling through her tears. "Yes."

"Thank you. For loving me. For forgiving me for being such a self-centered jerk and… We'll add a line to the vows when we repeat them. We'll put in there that each day, every day, we'll declare our love."

"Oh, my, I'm going to cry again. That is so romantic, so beautiful. I love you, David Westport."

David got to his feet and lifted Sandra into his arms, causing her to gasp in surprise, then laugh in delight.

"I'm not the featherweight I once was," she said, encircling his neck with her arms. "We're going to feel pretty silly if you hurt your back or something."

"I'm tough," he said, smiling at her. "Not macho. I don't ever want to hear that word again because it has gotten me in a whole lot of trouble."

"Well, now that you've got me captured here, what do you plan to do with me?"

"Keep you." He brushed his lips over hers. "Forever. That's the long range plan. But at this moment I'm going to make love to you."

"Oh, good," Sandra said, beaming, then kissed him with such intensity that David sank back onto the sofa, nestling her onto his lap.

The kiss went on and on, sending and receiving messages of forgiveness, of greater understanding, of love deep and rich and real.

David tightened his hold on Sandra, causing her breasts to crush against his chest in a sweet pain that sent heated sensations rocketing throughout her. Their breathing became labored as their passion soared.

David broke the kiss and spoke close to Sandra's moist lips.

"I think…" He cleared his throat. "I think we'd better stop for a second before one of the kids decides to wander out here for a drink of water or something."

"Mmm," Sandra said dreamily.

David stood again with Sandra in his arms and carried her to the bedroom. He set her on her feet, then turned on the small lamp on the nightstand to cast a golden glow over the room.

Desire engulfed them, began to burn, pulse and swirl within them, and they flung their clothes this way and that, not carrying where they landed. David swept back the blankets and they moved onto the bed, hands reaching eagerly for the other.

He drew her close, then kissed her with such heartfelt meaning it stole the very breath from her body and dispelled the haunting fears from her heart and mind, crushing them into dust.

They touched, then caressed, explored as though it was their very first time together, yet rejoicing, too, in the familiar that was theirs alone. They waited, anticipated, letting the passion build to a fever pitch.

And when they could bear no more, they became one. An entity so perfectly matched as the rocking rhythm began it was impossible to tell where one body ended and another began. When they were flung into oblivion seconds apart they called the name of the other, the one they would love so deeply...heart, mind, body and soul for the remainder of their days.

Then Sandra slept, tucked close to David's side, a soft, womanly smile still on her lips. He inched away from her to leave the bed and turned off the lamp. Then he opened the curtains just enough to allow moonlight to cascade over her like a silvery waterfall.

He slipped into the bed again and with a heart nearly bursting with gratitude and love, he watched his beloved Sandra sleep.

Chapter Thirteen

The next morning Molly entered the kitchen, then stopped and planted her hands on her pajama-clad hips.

"Oh, yuck," she said, frowning. "Gross. You're too old to be doing that stuff." She rolled her eyes heavenward. "This is so-o-o not cool, just totally embarrassing."

Sandra and David slowly and reluctantly ended the kiss they had been sharing and stepped apart, both turning to look at their scowling daughter.

"My dear child," David said, his voice slightly gritty, "I'll have you know that I love your mother very much. When two people love each other they express those feelings in various ways, one of which is a kiss."

"Not in front of your impressionable child," Molly said, nearly yelling.

"Get used to it, kid," David said.

Michael shuffled into the kitchen, appearing rumpled and sleepy.

"Michael," Molly said, "I caught Dad kissing Mom like in the movies right here in the kitchen."

"So what?" he said, yawning as he slid onto a chair at the table. "What do you want him to do? Smack her with a two-by-four? Parents kiss each other even when they're old, dim bulb."

"I don't think it's approximate," Molly said, poking her nose in the air. She frowned in the next instant. "Is that the right word?"

"I think you want to say *appropriate*," Sandra said, laughing, "and it is…appropriate for people in love to kiss each other. Yes, yes, even in front of their indignant children."

"I'm not indignant," Michael said, "I'm hungry."

"That's my boy," David said, chuckling. "He has his priorities in order and he's sticking to them. I am off to Westport's Emporium, family. By the way, if we can get a sitter, your mom and I are going out to dinner tonight. Just the two of us. Molly, close your eyes. I'm about to kiss your mother goodbye."

* * *

Sandra was able to get one of the teenagers on the street to agree to sit for the twins that evening and made a quick call to David at the store to tell him.

"Good show," David said. "A romantic dinner out with no kids. Do you think that's approximate?"

"No," Sandra said, laughing, "but it's definitely appropriate."

When she hung up the receiver she pressed her hands to her cheeks and blinked away tears of joy.

She was so happy, she thought, making no attempt to hide her smile. David loved her, just as she loved him. All her doubts and fears had been erased like chalk from a blackboard, or rather a greenboard like the twins had at school. She had been making herself miserable for so long for no reason.

Well, in all fairness to herself, David had given her cause to doubt his love by not expressing his feelings for her. Oh, it didn't matter whose fault it might have been, everything was fine now, just wonderful. She and David were going to grow old and creaky together in the years to come, despite the fact that their children thought they already were old and creaky.

Sandra looked heavenward, said a silent thank-you, then washed the kitchen floor as she counted down the hours until her *date* with her husband.

* * *

As the day progressed, David found himself glancing often at his watch. The knot in his stomach tightened as the hours ticked away, bringing him closer to the private dinner with Sandra.

Get it together, he told himself. He was working himself into a state of being just shy of a nervous breakdown. He had to stay calm and cool so he could explain things in a sensible manner to Sandra about... What would she say? How would she feel? What would she do?

He looked at his watch again.

Sandra chose a pretty pale pink sundress for the evening out. She'd taken a bubble bath, shampooed her hair and spritzed on cologne.

David dashed in the door after turning over the store to Eleanor Roosevelt Capelli and headed for the shower. He appeared in the living room wearing a gray suit, pale blue shirt and gray tie.

"Hi, Ashley," he said, to the baby-sitter.

"Hi, Mr. Westport," the teenager said.

"Ready to go, Sandra?" David said. "You look beautiful, by the way."

"Uh-oh, uh-oh," Molly said, jumping up and down. "He's going to kiss Mom again, I can tell. Don't look, Ashley, it's really embarrassing."

"You're cuckoo, kiddo," Ashley said, shaking her

head. "I'd be thrilled if my dad kissed my mom. All he does is yell...about everything."

"But they're old," Molly whispered. "My parents are ancient."

"Double cuckoo," Ashley said, laughing. "My brother is about the same age as your parents. You want to see antique folks? Take a look at *my* mom and dad."

"Oh," Molly said, flopping onto the sofa in a huff.

"Dim bulb," Michael said, shaking his head.

"As fascinating as all this is," David said, "it's time for us to hit the road. Sandra?"

"I'm ready, David," she said, "but... Well, honey, don't you think you should put on your shoes?"

"What?" David looked down at this sock-clad feet. "Oh, for Pete's sake."

As David sprinted back to the bedroom for his shoes, Sandra frowned.

He's nervous, she thought. He's a falling-apart-by-inches wreck. Why? *Now* what was on that complicated mind of his? No, she wasn't going to get herself all in a dither by speculating on what was upsetting him. She'd just wait and see what he had to say. Providing, of course, that he shared it with her. Oh, darn it, she wanted, needed, this evening to be special.

The usual instructions were given to Ashley regarding the twins bedtime, what was eligible for a snack and which television programs they were allowed to watch.

"Got it," Ashley said. "Have a nice evening."

Oh, I hope so, Sandra thought, as she and David left the house.

David had told Sandra they were not going to an Italian restaurant as it was definitely time for a change in cuisine. He'd selected a medium-priced establishment that offered a variety, including seafood and steaks. It was classy enough to have a romantic atmosphere, but within their budget as evidenced by the fact the prices were shown on both his and Sandra's menus.

David ordered a steak and baked potato and Sandra chose shrimp scampi. Red wine accompanied their meal.

"To us," David said, lifting his wineglass in a toast. "Forever and always."

Sandra smiled, touched her glass to his and they each took a sip.

They chatted about the weather, Molly's funny and endearing reaction to witnessing their kiss as well as Michael's "so what" attitude about it, and sundry other topics of little importance.

After their meals had been placed in front of them and they'd eaten enough to take the edge off their appetites, David took a deep breath and let it out slowly.

"I want to talk to you about something important, Sandra."

"Oh?" she said, raising her eyebrows. "Is this

something you're about to share the reason you forgot to put on your shoes?"

David nodded. "Yes."

"Well, that part is good. I was afraid you weren't planning on telling me what has you so uptight. Okay, David, I'm listening."

"Right." He drained his wine glass. "Well, it's about the empty building attached to the store. You know, the idea of buying it and punching through the wall to enlarge Westport's Emporium and, hopefully, increasing our income even after making the mortgage payment."

Sandra nodded, her gaze riveted on David.

"I believe that it would be a sound business venture for us, Sandra. There's lots of areas of the store than can be expanded and new things added, as well. It could give us some financial security down the line."

Sandra nodded again.

David fiddled with his spoon for a few seconds, then looked at her again.

"The thing is," he continued, "I don't want to do it."

Sandra frowned. "You're confusing me, David. You just made a great sales pitch for the plan and now you're saying... Did I miss something?"

"I'm getting to it," he said, then pulled the knot of his tie down a half an inch. "Remember the night I said I was going back to the store after dinner but I didn't, wasn't there when you phoned?"

"How could I forget?" she said dryly.

"Well, what I was really doing was driving to the other side of town where the tenements are. I saw and talked to the kids hanging out on the street." David smiled slightly. "The Street Corner Crew, that's what I call them in my mind." He shook his head. "God, Sandra, they have absolutely nothing. There's no summer sports programs for them, no money for equipment to play anything during the school year. Nothing. And people wonder why the kids in that neighborhood get in trouble."

"Are you talking about North End kids?" she said, then took another bite of her dinner.

"Yes, and that makes me angry. The North End is the North End. It shouldn't include the haves and the have-nots. All the kids should have the same opportunities, no matter what the income of their parents might be."

"I agree with you, David, but I'm still confused. One minute you're talking about expanding, then not expanding the emporium, and now the topic is North End kids who hang out on street corners. What's the connection? I assume there is one."

"Yeah, there is," he said, lifting his fork, then plunking it back onto his plate. "I want…I want the empty building next to the emporium to be a sports center for North End kids. *All* of them that want to come, from every neighborhood, nobody left out.

That, Sandra, would be my passing of the baton to pay back the gift I received from the benefactor."

"You…you want us to try to get a mortgage to buy that building so it can be…"

"No, no," he said, waving one hand in the air. "We'd have to do a massive fund-raising thing to be able to purchase the building, the equipment we need, the whole enchilada. What it would mean to us, our family, is that Westport's Emporium would have no opportunity to grow because the space wouldn't be available anymore. We, nor our children, would ever have more than we have now. We'd always be pinching pennies and Molly couldn't get pink braces and…"

"David," Sandra interrupted, smiling, "we're fine as we are. Just fine. The twins have a lot more than the kids you're telling me about. It's time to even things up in the North End. You have my complete support."

"Ah, man, I love you so much. I don't deserve you, but I'm sure going to keep you." David paused. "It's going to be a lot of work to get the money we need. That's why I got those guys to coach the teams I was in charge of, to free up my extra time. I'll give speeches to service groups, form a committee to plan fund-raisers, and…"

"I can push the whole idea in the *North End News*. Keep it right in front of people with my articles in the newspaper."

"Yeah," he said, nodding, "that's a great idea. I figure in the winter we'd have inside stuff. You know, Ping-Pong, chess, darts, jump rope...that fancy kind where they use two and three ropes at once.

"There would be room at one end to make a narrow basketball setup for practicing free throws and three-point shots, doing a little offense-defense drills and what have you. We might even have room for a baseball batting cage. There's a lot of space in that building."

"We could have knitting, crocheting, craft classes, too," Sandra said, her eyes sparkling. "There's that group of women at church who meet and make things for the bazaar. I wonder if they'd be willing to teach kids how to do all that? And there are so many retired people around here, David. Couldn't they take turns volunteering their time to supervise, make sure the kids don't kill each other?"

"Yeah, yeah, I like that," David said, his mind racing. "Later, after things are running smoothly, we could form actual teams with uniforms, keep those street corner kids busy in the summer. Ah, honey, it could be so good, give so much to so many."

"Yes," she said, smiling at him warmly. "You know, I was so angry at the benefactor because he wanted to be paid back for his gifts in the form of the passing of the baton. What I didn't realize is he is a very wise man. It has been a long time since I've seen you so excited, so filled with enthusiasm for a goal, a dream."

"And we'll do it together," he said. "The whole Westport family. If the twins want to play Ping-Pong there, then they can help with car washes, bake sales, rummage sales and on and on to help this all come true."

Sandra nodded.

"It's going to take tons of money just to buy the equipment we need," David said, frowning. "I don't know. Maybe I'm not being realistic to think we can raise the funds to buy that building. I want a sign all the way across the front of it that says The Street Corner Crew Club." He shook his head. "What we need is a fairy godmother like Cinderella. A rich one."

"Or…" Sandra said, leaning forward, "a…benefactor."

"What?"

"Think about it, David. That man gave you a full scholarship to Saunders. He gave gifts to enough others, even though we don't know the exact number who received them, to warrant a reunion, for heaven's sake. This is not a man who cuts food coupons out of the Sunday newspaper. Maybe *he'd* buy the building and donate it to The Street Corner Crew Club."

"It's a little hard to plead our case when we don't even know who he is."

"Professor Harrison is aware of his identity. You and

I will sit down and write a proposal, very fancy, very official, and ask the benefactor to buy the building.

"We outline the plans to raise the money for the equipment and what ongoing events we'd have to enable us to pay for the utilities and what have you.

"Plus, we'd say we are going to ask different service groups to take over a specific area. You know, the Breakfast Rotary would be approached about funding the baseball batting cage and blah, blah, blah. Get the drift? Then we ask Professor Harrison to take the proposal to the benefactor, making it clear that it's David Westport's way of passing the baton."

"Man, you're brilliant."

"I know," Sandra said, laughing merrily. "Kind of knocks you out, doesn't it? This lumpy body and brains, too. Awesome."

"You *are* awesome." David paused. "Hey, humor me here. I want you to sleep on all this because it would have a big impact on our lives. It means we'll never have fancy vacations or spiffy clothes, and we'll be applying for student loans to get our twins through college. We could have more, much more if we bought that building and expanded Westport's Emporium. I really need to know that you haven't been caught up in my enthusiasm for this thing and then wake up tomorrow morning and say…"

"What, no Lexus? Forget it, bubba." Sandra reached over and placed her hand on David's cheek.

"Oh, David, I won't change my mind. The Street Corner Crew Club is going to become a reality, no matter how long it takes. We're going to make it happen."

David grasped her hand and kissed the palm.

"Thank you," he said, his voice rough with emotion. "I love you, Sandra."

They smiled at each other, warm smiles, loving smiles, smiles that spoke of greater understanding, of a dream they would pursue together, united through all the ups and downs of what it would take to achieve their goal. It was a forever smile.

The waiter appeared at the table and asked if everything was to their satisfaction.

"Oh, yeah," David said, "and then some."

"Very good, sir," he said, then moved on.

"You'd better eat, David," Sandra said. "You've hardly touched your dinner."

David chuckled. "You're right. I only had one bite of the meal I ordered when I was with Professor Harrison. I'm not letting this steak go to waste."

"You know," Sandra said thoughtfully, "Kathryn Price might have experience in public relations, maybe know how special events are put together for raising funds and what have you. She would have seen all that done as a sought-after model, don't you think?

"Maybe she... No, perhaps not. Rachel only got a quick glimpse of her that one time on campus, but it was enough to know that something has happened to Kathryn that resulted in a disfigurement of some sort. That's so sad when you realize she made her living out of being beautiful."

"Well, it's a good thought," David said. "She would still have the knowledge. It would depend on where her head is after whatever it is that happened to her. Maybe she'd be open to a new challenge, be willing to share what she knows about organized events and stuff like that."

"Oh, goodness, my mind is going in a hundred directions at once," Sandra said. "Like one of the twins' Ping-Pong balls. I'm going to start making lists or I'll go on circuit overload. What about a grant? Don't they have grants for nonprofit endeavors?"

David shrugged. "I have no idea. If the benefactor would buy the building, the service groups purchase the equipment, then a grant would take the pressure off as far as maintaining the building, paying utilities, getting uniforms when we get to the baseball, basketball, soccer teams stage, buy bus passes to get those tenement kids over to our neighborhood and…

"You're right. Circuit overload. We're definitely going to make lists. But right now I'm going to eat this steak and thank the powers that be that you're my wife and you love me as much as I love you. Have you given any thought to renewing our vows?"

"I think," Sandra said slowly, "we'll do that when we've been married twenty years."

"But…"

"I'm serious, David. Knowing you want to do it means so much to me and that's enough for now. All the energy and money it would take to put that together, invite people, have a reception, can be better spent concentrating on passing the baton which is our first order of business. Okay?"

"On our twentieth anniversary?"

"Yes."

"Well," David said, laughing, "the twins think we're old and creaky now so they'll figure they'll be pushing us in wheelchairs to the altar by then, but it sounds good to me. Twenty years, then twenty more after that. Forever years, Sandra. The two of us."

"Yes. But we will repeat our vows quietly when we're home alone very soon, David. The first time we did that we were so young, were getting ready to become parents, give birth to miracles and see what the future would bring.

"This is almost like starting all over again with new goals and dreams. We're going to give birth to The Street Corner Crew Club, make certain that all the kids in the North End are treated equally, have a chance to have old-fashioned fun even if they don't excel at anything that is offered.

"But, oh, David, think of it. What a marvelous gift it would be to those who do have natural athletic talent and no way to develop it. They'd have a chance at something that was out of their reach before. By doing this, we can really make a difference, honey, open doors because we'll provide the keys."

"I do believe, my sweet," David said, "that that's what the benefactor had in mind. We were so angry with him at first, but now it makes sense. Paying back the gift. Passing the baton. Yeah, it makes sense."

Sandra nodded. "Even though we're going to spend a great deal of time putting our proposal together I still want to go to Saunders on the days I promised Rachel I'd drive in. We're not one bit closer to finding out who the benefactor is and I promised her I'd continue to help with the files we're going through."

"Sure, no problem." David laughed. "I definitely want you to discover the identity of the benefactor, only now I want to shake his hand, instead of punching him in the nose. Go figure."

"Actually there's more to our going through the files than just trying to discover who the benefactor is. Rachel is convinced that the board of directors at Saunders is harassing Professor Harrison about something, especially that creepy Alex Broadstreet. She feels there may be a clue to that situation in the files, too.

"I'd also like to know," Sandra continued, narrowing her eyes, "who that man is, the one who gave me the handkerchief with the *W* on it. I just can't shake the feeling that I have met him before, and I believe he's somehow connected to the reunion. I'm going to keep watch for him when I'm on campus. I'll also be on the lookout for Kathryn Price. Neither Rachel nor I have seen her since Rachel got that quick glimpse. Goodness, there's so much going on all of a sudden."

"Life ain't dull, my dear," David said, smiling.

"No, but life," Sandra said, unexpected tears of joy filling her eyes, "is good, my darling husband."

David nodded, then looked beyond Sandra's shoulder.

"Uh-oh," he said, "here comes temptation in its purest form."

"Let me guess," Sandra said, laughing. "A dessert cart."

"Got it in one, and there's a piece of black forest cake calling my name."

They ended up sharing the rich dessert, each savoring forkfuls of the gooey offering. Sandra finally admitted she was full and couldn't eat another bite.

"Oh, a man's work is never done," David said, sliding the plate toward him. "I'll sacrifice myself and finish this off."

"Big of you, I must say." Sandra paused. "You know, David, we're just an ordinary couple doing our thing, as the saying goes. Or we were, until the existence of the benefactor was made known to us by Professor Harrison. Now? We're suddenly caught up in mysteries, so many unanswered questions."

"Yep," David said, nodding. "Who is the benefactor? And why is the board harassing Gilbert Harrison? It can't just be because he's a little old-fashioned in the way he operates."

David polished off the last bite of the cake.

"And moving right along," he said. "Will the benefactor like our proposal and buy that building for The Street Corner Crew Club?" He smiled. "Will Molly ever forgive us because she'll have ordinary braces on her teeth instead of pink ones?"

"See what I mean?" Sandra said, leaning forward. "It's like living in the middle of a Agatha Christie novel all of a sudden. So many, many questions."

"All of which will eventually have answers," David said. But there is one thing we know, one thing that's etched in stone."

"There is?"

"Oh, yes, ma'am. We know, Mrs. Westport, that we are deeply in love with each other and always will be. We know that to be true in our hearts, our minds, our very souls. We know how blessed we are to have each other and our dynamite children. We know we have forever love."

Sandra smiled at him, the love he spoke of shining in her eyes.

"Yes," she said.

And because the expression on David's face and in his eyes matched her own, she knew that was all she needed to say.

* * * * *

Look for the next book in the new
Special Edition continuity
MOST LIKELY TO...
THE BEAUTY QUEEN'S MAKEOVER
by reader-favorite
Teresa Southwick

When high-profile defense attorney Nate Williams comes face-to-face with his college crush, Kathryn Price, he must come to terms with the secret he's kept to himself for years—one that could destroy any chance they have for happiness.

Available August 2005 wherever
Silhouette Books are sold.

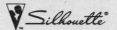
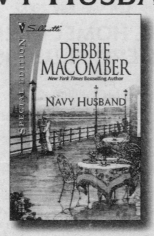

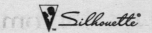

If you enjoyed what you just read,
then we've got an offer you can't resist!

Take 2 bestselling love stories FREE!

Plus get a FREE surprise gift!